About the Author

Jessika resides in beautiful Grand Rapids, Michigan with her exceptionally fluffy cat, Bones. When she's not writing, she enjoys reading, movies, and hiking. She holds a love for bees and turtles. She is also an enthusiastic environmentalist and supports the preservation of our beautiful planet.

The Bonds of Glory

Jessika Mahler

The Bonds of Glory

Olympia Publishers
London

www.olympiapublishers.com
OLYMPIA PAPERBACK EDITION

Copyright © Jessika Mahler 2023

The right of Jessika Mahler to be identified as author of
this work has been asserted in accordance with sections 77 and 78 of
the Copyright, Designs and Patents Act 1988.

All Rights Reserved

No reproduction, copy or transmission of this publication
may be made without written permission.
No paragraph of this publication may be reproduced,
copied or transmitted save with the written permission of the publisher,
or in accordance with the provisions
of the Copyright Act 1956 (as amended).

Any person who commits any unauthorised act in relation to
this publication may be liable to criminal
prosecution and civil claims for damage.

A CIP catalogue record for this title is
available from the British Library.

ISBN: 978-1-80439-009-2

This is a work of fiction.
Names, characters, places and incidents originate from the writer's
imagination. Any resemblance to actual persons, living or dead, is
purely coincidental.

First Published in 2023

Olympia Publishers
Tallis House
2 Tallis Street
London
EC4Y 0AB

Printed in Great Britain

Dedication

I dedicate this book to my sister, Autumn, my very own Adridia.

Prologue

The bedroom was dark, save for the dying fire in the hearth, casting eerie shadows all across the room. A woman dozed in her grand canopy bed, a book open on her stomach, her dark hair splayed out over the silk pillow. A princess stood over her mother's bed, gazing at her still youthful face, her eyes aglow with something sinister. The empress awoke and sat up suddenly, her hand clutching her heart, startled at her daughter standing over her.

"Sinisstra, what are you doing?" she asked, running a hand through her unruly mass of curls. Her daughter's hands curled into fists.

"You're weak," she whispered, working up the courage to do what she so badly wanted to do. There was something in her, driving her, pushing her. She could feel it writhing in her chest, wrapping around her heart, invading her soul.

"Did you drink wine before you went to bed? You know that always makes your head fuzzy." The empress laid back down, completely unaware that her daughter was no longer in control of her own body. "Go back to bed, darling, we'll talk in the morning."

"No," Sinisstra snarled, her voice strained.

Her mother sat up once again and gazed at her daughter, wondering where she got the audacity to defy her. "I am your empress and mother, you will do as I say. What has gotten into you?"

"You're weak." The princess was no longer whispering. "You are weak and you let the other kingdoms walk all over you. You are unworthy of the throne. I could do better than you. I could change the course of history." Sinisstra's voice became more steady as she spoke and her hands no longer shook. "The empire doesn't respect you. They don't fear you as they should, as they once did." She approached the bed. "You don't deserve the throne, you aren't worthy of it," she repeated. "But I am going to fix it. I'm going to fix everything. It's just a pity you won't be able to see it."

"Sinisstra?" Her mother reached for her but hesitated, wary of her daughter. Sinisstra lunged. "Guar-" Her cry for help was cut off when her daughter grabbed the back of her head, gripping her hair in a closed fist to force her head back, and shoved something down her throat. The princess stepped back as the empress began convulsing, blood leaking out of her ears, nose, and mouth. She reached for her daughter, the book she had fallen asleep reading falling to the floor, the pages tearing. Sinisstra shut her eyes against the image. A few more choking noises escaped her lips before she breathed her final breath. The princess opened her eyes and smiled darkly at the silence. She stepped forward and rested a gentle hand on her mother's cheek, slick with blood, before her features were overcome with absolute grief and she threw herself over her mother's body, wailing loudly.

The door slammed open as guards rushed in. "She's dead!" Sinisstra cried, tears sliding down her cheeks. "Someone poisoned her!" She cradled her mother's head in her hands, her fingers covered in blood as she looked up at the guards, allowing anger to seep into her features. "I swear to you and the rest of the empire, I will avenge her death."

She bent over her mother's body again, pressing a sickly-sweet kiss to her forehead, before stepping away to allow the healers to work, her lips coated with her mother's blood.

"Princess, you should get to your chambers, especially if a killer is on the loose." One of her handmaidens led her out into the hallway as the princess smiled darkly to herself, the ring of the empress clutched in her hand.

Chapter 1

Jerylia

The princess of Serradon approached the rotting wooden door, her armor clicking with every movement. She turned to the group of people following her as she pulled her sword out of its sheath, the metal glinting in the setting sunlight. "Let's make this quick. My mother is hosting a feast tonight." She grinned and kicked the door in, wooden splinters flying.

The men that had been playing cards in the main room scattered like rodents as the princess shattered the hinges on the door. She rolled her shoulders and spun her sword in a quick circle, a manic grin present on her lips. The group split, the two archers planting themselves in the doorway to prevent escape before they started shooting at the escaping thieves, their bows singing. The princess ducked through another doorway, into a room with a long wooden table inhabiting the center and a large hearth at either end. Two men ran at her, swords raised, like idiots, but she quickly disposed of them with two fierce swipes of her sword. She sighed, yanking her blade out of a ribcage, admiring the crimson blood dripping from the once clean metal. Green streaks of magic whipped past her. She turned to see the witch, the woman's eyes glowing as she cast her spells.

"They could at least make it a challenge," the princess mumbled, shrugging her shoulders. The witch grinned at her, green magic wreathing her wrists and arms. The princess peered around the room again, spotting a shallow doorway next to one of the hearths. "Not very good at hiding, are you?" she muttered to herself as she hoisted her sword once again, ducking into the doorway. She barely registered the punch to her ribs as a man sprung out of an alcove in the hallway. She plunged her sword into his abdomen and swiftly pulled it out again, relishing his scream while allowing him to fall to the floor on his knees. "Oh, shut up. You're the moron who didn't run when you saw me coming." She slid her dagger from its sheath on her thigh and slid it across his throat. His screams died and she continued, the petite witch not far behind. They only met three more men in the hallway, all of which were easily put down, before they came to a room with a single table in the center and a straw bed in the corner. The small leather pouches of gold tipped over on the table gave enough away about the occupants of the abandoned cellar. There was most definitely illegal activity happening here, which was good for the princess and her squadron. A tall, lanky man was trying to scrape the gold coins into a large burlap sack but quickly stopped when the princess entered the room.

"Well, this is disappointing. I was expecting someone, well, I'm going, to be honest here." The princess motioned to the man with her sword. "I was expecting someone a lot hotter than you. You mean to tell me that you are the King of Thieves, a very pretentious nickname, by the way." She stalked closer to him with every word, until she stood directly in front of him, the point of her sword under his chin.

"I could say the same thing, Jerylia 'Foebreaker'," he snarled. His arm moved, quicker than the princess realized he was capable of, and he attempted to thrust a knife between her armor plates. She thrust up with her sword, the sharpened metal piercing his skull and brain with ease.

"Dumbass." She heard movement behind her and turned, yanking the sword from his body.

"That's him?" Adridia asked, an eyebrow raised.

"Nope. There is no way. I'll bet you five gold pieces he was a decoy." She kicked his lifeless body, rolling him onto his back. The warrior grinned, the blood splattering across her face making her look almost insane.

"I know better than to bet against you and your gut feelings." Jerylia snorted as she gathered up the gold pieces on the central table.

"Why not? We just got paid." She shook the bag, the gold clinking together.

"Can we please go? I'm starving!" The two women laughed when Faryn's shout echoed through the decrepit hideout.

The great hall was filled with noise. The queen sat at her table on a dais, her consort, Jerylia's father, next to her, whispering in her ear while she laughed. Several loud crashes, almost like the sound of two people wearing armor clashing, were heard in the hallway before the large doors were thrust open, revealing the princess, her face and armor splattered with blood. She raised her fist, the head of the King of Thieves dangling from it by his hair.

"Another victory for Jerylia 'Foebreaker' Serra, warrior princess of Serradon!" The tall blonde woman coming up behind her announced to the crowded hall. The people cheered as a servant came and took the head from her along with her armor, leaving her in a black tunic and tight black pants. She wore a shit-eating grin as the cheers echoed through the stone castle. She was vaguely aware of her companions removing their armor as well as she raised her arms and reveled in the glory of yet another victory. The real King of Thieves may yet live, but his operation was in shambles. They had dealt a crippling blow.

"Someone bring me a needle and a ring!" she shouted into the crowd. Another servant came forward bearing a needle and a small metal ring. The princess handed them to her blonde companion before sweeping her hair back to reveal a row of silver rings on her right ear. She knelt and held her breath, bracing for the prick of the needle. She felt the needle pierce the tough cartilage, almost near the tip, hissing at the sharp pain radiating through her ear, and the small ring slid through. She could fit two more rings on the right ear before she would have to switch to the left one. She stood and raised her sword to the ceiling, prompting a thunderous cheer from the crowd.

"I have to speak to my mother but you'd better save me a pint," she said to her squadron, pinning them each with a look that promised death if they didn't.

"Absolutely not. If there's alcohol sitting there, it won't be for long," one of the archers told her, a grin on his face. She gave him an obscene gesture before making her way to the dais where her mother sat.

"Did you kill the King of Thieves? I'm still not sure," her father said from the queen's side.

"No, this is just a new look I'm trying out." She gestured to the blood drying on her face before snatching a small roasted potato off of his plate. He only smiled at her and shook his head, his eyes warm.

"I'm proud of you for accomplishing such a feat," her mother said, sipping at her wine.

"It was easier than expected. He certainly didn't look like he deserved that absolutely ridiculous title. Something about it doesn't feel right." The princess snapped at a servant scurrying past. "Bring me a plate, extra helping of potatoes, with a pint of that extra strong ale and I'll add a few extra silvers to your purse." The servant nodded before continuing to the kitchen. "I'm going to keep looking into it, but I wanted to do it without the public watching my every move. I'm going to earn this earring, don't worry." She brushed her hand over her ear, wincing at the soreness of the new addition.

"Do what you need to do, Jerylia. I trust you to do what's best for the kingdom." The queen smiled but it didn't quite reach her eyes. The princess knew the queen missed the warrior's life. Her mother had married at twenty-six, the expected age for marriage, but hadn't given birth to Jerylia until she was almost three hundred years old. All so she could continue adventuring.

"Thank you, my Queen," the princess mocked, earning a laugh from her father before she turned to join her squadron at their table near the huge windows. She nearly ran over the servant girl carrying her plate and ale. "Thank you." She pressed a few silver coins into the servant's hand as she took her plate and mug.

"The warrior princess returns," Adridia called from her place on the bench, raising her foaming mug towards the ceiling. Jerylia grinned and puffed out her chest, smashing her cup against Adridia's before they both drank deeply from them. The princess wiped the liquid from her face with her sleeve as she sat on the bench next to the witch. The warrior and the twin archers sat across from them at the table.

"What did your mother say about it?" Gwera leaned over and asked.

"We have her permission to continue earning our victory," Jerylia told her squadron.

"So, guess what I did last night," Faryn leaned in and asked, his breath smelling of ale.

"I thought the game was 'who did you do last night?'"

Adridia joked after loosing a loud belch.

"You aren't wrong. I may have slipped and my cock may have landed in a certain head seamstress." He grinned as he leaned over the table as if it was some secret. The seamstress had probably already told everyone in the castle. It was an honor to be laid by one of the Kaen twins. Theal was still quiet from where he sipped on his ale. He was just as skillful as his brother in the bedroom, though he was much less boastful about it.

"You are disgusting." Gwera wrinkled her nose at Faryn who was winking at some poor waif across the room.

"Hey, it's not my fault you can't enjoy the wonders of sex because you can't finish without setting beds on fire." The witch's cheeks flamed red. It was true, the witch had to proclaim celibacy after several incidents concerning fire and beds.

"You said you wouldn't mock me for that," she hissed at him.

"Fine, I won't mock you for that." He was quiet for a few more moments. "So did Jerylia finally get you that booster seat?" he asked her. Adridia laughed loudly as Gwera slammed her goblet down, wine sloshing over the sides.

"At least I don't try to fuck everything that moves!" She stood, shouting mere inches from his face. Theal was smiling from his corner of the table before his gaze shifted and landed on Adridia. It was no secret that the male elf was in love with the warrior, but she was oblivious, or at least she pretended to be. Jerylia and Adridia had spoken extensively of her predicament, so the princess knew Adridia also had feelings for the archer but used the excuse that she didn't want to ruin their friendship and subsequently ruin the dynamic of the squadron. So, she did the same thing he did, buried her feelings in other people, both males, and females, and just as successfully.

"Hey, Faryn." The female he had been eyeing from across the room approached the table, tucking a lock of strawberry blonde hair behind her ear, a blush on her cheeks. He winked at the rest of the group before bidding them a good night and stalking off with the woman. Theal followed suit soon after, with two women at his side.

"Damn, Theal can pull," Adridia announced, knocking back another pint. Jerylia eyed her carefully, knowing she would most likely want to find her own elf to bed. To bury the pain. Gwera stood as she noticed the hall begin to empty.

"He certainly can. I should get to bed too. I have some reading to do." Her cheeks went rosy as she brought up reading.

"Try not to set your bed on fire. No pleasure is worth having to listen to the head laundress complain about another set of charred sheets," Jerylia smirked at the witch.

"It only ever happened when I had sex with another person." She shrugged before leaving the hall, her red curls bouncing as she walked. Adridia pinned the princess with her gaze.

"So, your birthday is coming up," she said, trying to sound casual.

"Yeah, in a month," the princess replied, almost catching on to what the warrior was implying, and trying to ignore it.

"You'll have to get married. Have you thought about your suitors?" the blonde asked.

"Why are you bringing this up?" Jerylia gripped her mug harshly before bringing it to her lips, avoiding eye contact with the warrior.

"Listen, I wasn't going to say anything but your mother is going to be on you about it soon, so I figured I'd talk to you about it just in case, ya know and—"

"For the love of Serra just please spit it out," Jerylia

interrupted her friend's rambling.

"You should consider Faryn as a suitor," she blurted.

"Why would I do that?" The princess knew the answer, she just wanted to hear it out loud.

"Because he's in love with you, and he's been in love with you for a long time," Adridia answered. Jerylia shot up from the table, the bench scraping along the stone floor.

"I'm going to bed," she said curtly before she turned to walk away.

"Are you going to say anything to him about it?" Adridia called after her.

"Yeah, as soon as you say something to Theal," Jerylia spat. Adridia recoiled, the words finding their mark.

"This is not the same. I am not required a husband." The warrior was quiet, a rare occurrence. Jerylia leaned forward and placed her palms on the table.

"And the difference between you and me is that you return Theal's affections. Faryn should marry someone that loves him. He only wants me because I'm the one female he can't have. He's been saying since we were kids that he wants to marry a queen and, while he might not realize it, I would be his greatest conquest. That is why he wants me. Not to mention I'm fucking gorgeous." Adridia let out a short breathy laugh through her nose and the joke did nothing to sway her from the conversation as Jerylia had hoped it would.

"You could love him, in time." Jerylia pushed away from the table and folded her arms over her chest.

"Not in the way he wants me to. I have known him for almost twenty years. I hold nothing more than brotherly love towards him in my heart and because of that it grosses me out to think about sleeping with him."

"So, you'd take a love-filled future away from a foreign prince just so you wouldn't have to face your own guilt." The words dripped with judgment.

"You're insinuating that Faryn is the only person who could fall in love with me. I have no guilt about this. I value Faryn as a friend and I have never once led him on or hinted that we could be something more. You don't get to lecture me on my love life when you can't even control your own. Stop meddling with my affairs to keep your mind off of Theal. We are not in the same situation." Adridia was silent as she stared up at Jerylia. The princess was disappointed in the warrior. All she'd wanted to do tonight was celebrate her victory with the people she loved most and now her head was clouded with anger. They were both drunk and most likely wouldn't remember this the next day but at this moment, the blonde's words were knives. "I need time to think." The princess didn't hear what else the warrior said as she pushed through the small crowd still celebrating in the doorway and entered the hallway.

She entered her room and shut the thick wooden door shut behind her, leaning against it as she sighed heavily. Her eyelids were heavy as she removed her bloodstained clothing and fell into bed, moaning at the feel of the soft blankets against her bare skin. She curled on her side and clutched a pillow to her stomach before slipping into sweet oblivion.

"Jerylia Serra!" She heard her mother call through her rooms from her place in her steaming bathtub. She groaned and slid further into the warm bath water, hoping it would swallow her up.

"Busy, come back later!" the princess called back to her mother. She knew the queen was here to talk about her impending marriage and she was far too hungover to get started with that conversation. She was still stewing from her conversation with Adridia last night that she, surprisingly, still remembered, though it was hazy.

"Not so fast, you and I need to have a conversation about your marriage." The queen stepped into the bathroom, bringing with her an air of regality that definitely didn't belong in Jerylia's clothes-strewn bathing room. "I let you off the hook last night by not bringing it up at the feast so we are going to talk about it now." The princess groaned and sunk further into the water. Maybe she could just drown herself to get out of it.

"What about it? I don't want to marry a prince from another country. I don't want to marry anyone," she said stubbornly, folding her arms under the surface of the water, like a stubborn child.

"Well, that's too bad. You haven't yet chosen another suitor and have made no plans to do so. So I took the liberty of inviting the three princes to stay with us until your birthday."

"Mother!" Jerylia shouted before groaning loudly again.

"I wasn't finished." The queen composed herself. "The princes arrive today and you are to greet them when they arrive." She turned to leave before pausing and glancing around the room, then at her daughter. "And you will be dressed appropriately."

Chapter 2

Jerylia

The princess bounced on her toes as she stood in the grand entrance to the castle. Her mother had forced her into a split riding skirt over leggings and a loose white shirt with a wide collar that exposed her collarbones underneath a tight, black embroidered corset. Her handmaidens had yanked and twisted her hair back into a long braid that now rested on her shoulder, tickling her neck. Adridia and Gwera stood by her side in full armor, one a comforting presence and one a mild annoyance. Her stomach twisted as the large doors began to open, a small crowd of people behind them.

"Hello, your majesties." She did an awkward shallow curtsy, acknowledging their status above her. "If you'll follow me, we will make formal introductions in the throne room." They all nodded before she turned and began to walk towards the throne room. She was acutely aware of every royal scrutinizing her and her kingdom, judging every little detail.

"You forgot to smile," Gwera leaned over and whispered. Jerylia's cheeks reddened slightly and she shot her friend a cold look. She took a deep breath as well as she could in the corset, calming herself.

Her mother was perched on her throne, the carved wolves' heads at the top always snarling and the carved depiction of Serra combating them with her gentleness. The queen was dressed impeccably in a deep green gown decorated with curling vines over the bodice and hem. Her hair had been braided into a crown that held a glittering silver crown of metallic ivy, made by her father. The princess climbed the stone steps to sit on the smaller throne to the right of the queen's. The queen flashed them all a welcoming smile, warmth radiating from her eyes.

"It is the honor of Serradon to welcome you. We trust that your journey was pleasant." The queen turned to look at her daughter and grabbed her hand, her fingers cold from the chilled air. "It is my distinct pleasure to introduce you to Princess Jerylia Dwymeth Serra of Serradon, first and only born child of Queen Aselidda Dwymeth Serra of Serradon and Ariand Serra, blacksmith of the North." Jerylia sat up straight, rolling her shoulders back, unashamed, her spine protesting at the position. "Princess Jerylia boasts seven victories in battle and comes of age in a month's time. She has not declared a suitor yet." The princess scanned the small crowd of royals. The King of Fastille and his son stepped forward. The prince was tall and thin, with strawberry blonde hair and freckles dotting his cheeks.

"It is Fastille's honor to present my eldest son, Prince Adwor Fastren." The prince stepped forward and bowed slightly. Jerylia could see from her perch on her throne that his hands were shaking slightly.

"It is an honor to finally meet you. Your prowess in battle as well as your astounding beauty are legendary." Jerylia fought the urge to gag at the bootlicking. She kept a neutral expression on her face as she replied.

"The honor is mine." The Fastille royals stepped back, allowing the King and Queen of Saeroc to step forward, the prince between them. The western coast had been very kind to the prince, blessing him with tan skin and blonde hair. Days spent fishing in the sun had made him very muscular and he had an easy smile, one that told her he would probably not be a faithful husband. He was also the youngest of the princes, only eleven years older than herself.

"It is the honor of Saeroc to present our eldest son, Prince Haledin Sae." The prince bowed towards the queen and princess, winking.

"It is an honor to meet you, Princess. Your country is beautiful, much like yourself." The princess squirmed in her seat. She glanced at her mother, whose smile did not match the distaste in her eyes. The Saeroc royals stepped back and the Queen of Torith stepped forward with her son. He was tall and muscular, with a mop of black hair and sun-tanned skin. His smile was warm and a dimple appeared on his right cheek as he flashed his perfect teeth. Jerylia automatically knew he would be her prince, desire curling in her stomach. She forced herself not to return his smile, to avoid angering the other royals.

"It is the honor of Torith to present my eldest son, Prince Kaed Torra." Kaed placed a fist over his chest and bowed, a warrior's bow to another warrior. The princess smiled slightly.

"It would be an honor to hear some of your battle stories. I hear they are quite the tales, your highness." He looked up at her with warm brown eyes.

"It would be an honor to tell them to someone who hasn't heard them before." The royals chuckled, including her mother. The queen stood, her hands clasped together in front of her.

"A feast will be held tonight, in honor of your visit with us and we would be delighted to see you all there. Unfortunately, my daughter will not be available to socialize until then as she has important matters to attend to in the city." The princess was grateful for the pardon. She was already exhausted from having so many strangers stay with them. "But she would be happy to show you each to your separate wings of the castle before she leaves." Jerylia could have strangled her mother. Adridia snickered from her place just a few feet from the princess.

"Of course, if you'll follow me." She descended the stairs and exited the throne room, chest tight with anticipation. They passed the Great Hall, where feasts were held. She gestured to the grand doors at the entrance, intricately carved with depictions of some of the legends of Serra. "This is where we host our feasts but most nights dinner will be served to you in your rooms. You'll each have a small team of five servants standing by in case you need something," she explained. They walked along in silence for a time before they came to the first visitor's wing, decorated with orange flags depicting a hawk, the flag of Fastille. "This is where the Fastillian royal family will be staying for the duration of their visit." The king, queen, and prince emerged from the crowd of people in front of me followed by a few servants carrying large trunks of belongings.

"Please forgive me for sounding too forward, but it is customary in Fastille to kiss upon greeting. It is a way of gaining trust before beginning a conversation, especially when discussing betrothal." The prince told the princess before he entered his wing. Of course, she already knew that. While she may have been avoiding choosing a suitor, her mother made sure she learned all the customs of the foreign countries for diplomatic purposes. The princess hesitated but conceded, tilting her head up. Her entire body went cold the moment their lips touched and she pulled away suddenly, having never felt that before. The prince smiled down at her, clearly not feeling at all the same way. Jerylia smiled and nodded, fighting the urge to wipe the slimy feeling from her lips.

"I will see you at the feast tonight," she told him before leading the rest of the royals on to their quarters. They stopped at a hall decorated with blue flags depicting a leaping fish, the flag of Saeroc. "This is where the Saerocan royals will be staying." She gestured to the hallway. The king and queen rushed forward, their servants trailing in their wake. Prince Haledin strutted forward, stopping in front of the princess. She immediately regretted her decision to allow the Fastillian prince to kiss her because she knew the other two were going to ask the same thing of her.

"I would ask that the same courtesy be extended to me that was extended to the prince of Fastille." He flashed an easy smile at her, a crocodile's grin. For some reason she didn't quite trust this prince. Something about him that she couldn't quite put her finger on told her to run. Instead, she smiled and tilted her head up once again. His lips were soft when they touched hers, his tongue darting in between her lips quickly. The prince pulled back, flashed her a smile, and sauntered down the hallway. Jerylia returned his smile, with some degree of difficulty before she continued, stopping at yet another hallway, this one next to the hall that housed her own quarters. Green flags hung in this hallway with depictions of a stag in the center, the flag of Torith.

"This is where the Torithi royals will be housed." The prince sent his mother and father into the wing before turning towards the princess.

"Yes, you can have a kiss too." She interrupted before he could speak. He smiled at her, that gods-damned dimple appearing that would be the death of her.

"I was only going to ask if I could reserve an hour of your time after the feast tonight." Jerylia's cheeks reddened. "But I will accept that kiss."

He placed one hand on her arm and cupped her cheek with the other before lowering his mouth to hers. The instant their lips touched warmth spread through her all the way to her toes. She knew this is what it was supposed to feel like. He pulled away and hummed slightly, a mischievous smile plastered on his lips. He turned to walk away, his hands clasped behind his back.

"Yes!" she shouted after him. He turned back towards her, eyebrows raised. "Yes, you may reserve my time after the feast."

"I look forward to it." The tone of his voice sent butterflies into her stomach. He bowed his head before joining his parents.

"Don't say a word," the princess snapped to the warrior and the witch as she stalked to her bedroom. Adridia grinned and followed after her. The warrior began strapping the princess into her armor as quickly as possible, their fight from the previous night almost forgotten as the three women spoke of the three princes.

"I don't like that one from Saeroc. He has something off about him," Adridia commented as she did the ties on the breastplate.

"He's cute but he looks like he needs a personality." Gwera lounged on a small fainting couch as she watched the warrior work.

"That one from Fastille is so not your type," Adridia finished the breastplate and went to work on the leg plates, the thick metal fitting snugly over her thighs.

"I don't have a type. I've never been allowed to fraternize with men before, besides the twins."

"Oh, you have a type." Adridia looked up and grinned. "It's anyone who is physically able to throw you up against a wall." Jerylia's cheeks reddened and heat settled in her abdomen as an image popped into her mind of Kaed doing that exact thing to her.

"Gods-dammit now you've got me turned on," Gwera cackled from her sofa. "I like Kaed. He makes me feel some sort of way."

"And he looks like he would be able to throw you up against the wall."

"Stop talking about the wall, Adri, or we're not going anywhere because I'm going to have to stay here and take care of myself."

"You're allowed to do that?" Jerylia gave her an incredulous look.

"I'm the princess, I'm not dead. Gwera taught me how," she shrugged and pulled on her leather gloves and matching boots.

"You've corrupted her!" Adridia shouted dramatically, grabbing Jerylia's head and holding it to her chest. She pushed away from the warrior and smoothed her hair.

"Please, you've been talking about your sexual success for years now."

"That's different. I didn't teach you how to do it." She paused. "But isn't it amazing?" Jerylia smiled.

"Like a thousand suns all exploding at once."

"As much as I enjoy this conversation, we need to get going if we want to be back for the feast." Gwera stood, brushing off her simple witch's robe. Jerylia grabbed her sword, still in its scabbard, tying it around her hips as they walked at a quick pace through the castle. The twins were waiting for them at the main entrance.

"How did the meeting of the princes go this morning?" Theal asked, his deep green irises bright with curiosity. Adridia opened her mouth to say something before Jerylia interrupted her.

"It was fine. Nothing happened." She glared at the warrior

who grinned.

"Torith," Adridia blurted out before Jerylia could stop her. It was only one word but excitement buzzed through them anyway. Theal chuckled and shook his head while Faryn forced a smile at that.

"Can we please just go?" The princess groaned before pushing the door open.

The streets were crowded as people shopped the noon market. The princess and her companions ducked in and out of the taverns lining the streets, asking the whereabouts of the King of Thieves. They always received the same answer: "You took care of him yourself, your highness." The princess collapsed in a chair at The Thirsty Maiden, one of her favorite taverns in Serramor.

"Maybe we were wrong and that little weasel was indeed the real King of Thieves." Her companions sat around her, each with a pint in their hands.

"No way that skinny little twerp was the notorious criminal. It doesn't add up." Faryn shook his head, his eyes meeting Jerylia's. "We'll find him, Jer. We've only been looking for a few hours. This could take days."

She nodded and drank deeply from her cup. She heard a thump and lowered the mug to see a stranger sitting at their table. He took the princess' cup from her fingers and drank the rest of the ale in it, wiping a few stray drops from his beard. He had broad shoulders and muscular arms, scars littering the tanned skin. She also noticed his gut protruding from his profile, the kind you can only get from a lifetime of too much ale. This was the kind of man Jerylia had expected to be the King of Thieves. He leaned forward and grinned, showing yellowed teeth.

"I heard you were looking for me."

Chapter 3

Adridia

The warrior's heart thundered in her chest as she realized who was sitting across from her at the table. She eyed the princess warily, her hand creeping towards the sword sheathed at her hip. Jerylia only smiled at the criminal. Adridia groaned internally. The princess was always goading their adversaries into fights, it was what she was good at, even though her companions begged her to stop. It almost always got them into trouble.

"Now you look like someone who calls himself the King of Thieves. I'm going to tell you the same thing I told your decoy, it's a pretentious nickname," he chuckled darkly and shook his head slightly, leaning in to whisper to her.

"You should never have pursued me, Princess." The rest of the patrons in the bar stood, weapons already in their hands. The king himself had the front of Jerylia's shirt bunched in his hand with a dagger at her throat. The princess just laughed. Adridia reminded herself to speak with her friend about finding humor in the wrong situations. "I could kill you in a matter of seconds, what exactly do you find so funny?" he snarled in her face, spit flying from his lips.

"Because you threatened my safety and it is a really bad idea to do that with my friends around." She winked at Adridia and the blonde smiled before all the mugs of ale in the tavern exploded, the water in the ale controlled by the warrior. Green magic streaked around the room, crawling into the throats of the enemy patrons, choking them where they stood. Adridia was already swinging her sword towards a burly woman charging at her, the cool metal slicing open her stomach with ease. She didn't even flinch when warm blood splattered her face and armor. She turned to see a man bearing down on her but he quickly fell with an arrow through the eye, thanks to Theal's sharp reflexes. She nodded her thanks and twisted her hand, the ale floating in the air following her movement. It fell to the ground in a sticky splash, soaking their boots as they all whirled towards the center of the room when they heard Jerylia cry out, just in time to see her slash the King's throat.

Blood coated the princess as she heaved his body off of her.

"Can someone please take a look at this?" She propped her foot on a chair so they could see the dagger sticking out of her armor. The King of Thieves must have been strong to have been able to pierce the thick plates that covered her thighs. The armor had been made by her father who had proudly earned the title of the best blacksmith in Serradon. Gwera was at her side in an instant, magic probing under the armor to assess the damage. "It's just a flesh wound," Jerylia argued but the witch shut her up with a glare.

"I'll be the judge of that." She yanked the dagger out of the armor and quickly unstrapped the leg piece. "It's just a flesh wound," she announced and they all breathed a sigh of relief.

"I literally just said that," Jerylia argued. Gwera asked the bartender for some bandages and water before turning and pushing the princess into a chair.

"Yes, but you also said that when we fought those slave traders in Trayston when there was literally an arrow embedded in your shoulder," Faryn argued, already going to work unstrapping the rest of her armor. Her dark undershirt and leggings were soaked with blood and stray strands of her hair were sticking to her neck, matted in the blood.

"I still think I would have been fine."

"It was sticking out the other side!"

"You were in the infirmary for almost a week and you should have stayed longer," Theal agreed with his twin.

"Please, you guys are just worrywarts." They all gave her a pointed look. She folded her arms across her chest after Faryn removed the chest piece.

"You might want to change your clothes before the feast. Kaed might not find the whole 'I slit someone's throat and he bled all over me' look attractive," Adridia suggested. The princess waved her off.

"Then he doesn't have any business being married to me plus we don't have time. Bandage me up and then we have to go. My mother is going to kill me if I'm late." She glanced around the room impatiently. As soon as the bandage was secured, she was on her feet, limping out the door. "Last one to the castle has to see the princes to bed," she shouted behind her. Her companions scrambled to pick up her armor and chase after her down the street.

Faryn was the last of them to set foot over the threshold of the castle gates. Adridia grinned at him. "Make sure to kiss the princes goodnight, they seem to rather enjoy that," she jeered at him. He gave her an obscene gesture as he scowled which only seemed to make her laugh harder. They quickly handed off their armor to the servants waiting for them inside the doorway. The crowd in the Great Hall stared at them and their blood-spattered faces and clothes. Adridia grinned at the disgust the foreign royals wore on their faces.

"Didn't I tell you the princess would make an appearance, princes? She does enjoy making an entrance." The queen raised her crystal goblet as she winked at her daughter. The royal families wrinkled their noses at the blood-soaked fighters. Adridia kept her eye on Kaed since he seemed the most likely to become the one to win Jerylia's heart. He looked more intrigued than disgusted. "It seems she has yet another successful battle under her belt," she remarked as she lifted the wine to her lips.

"I was just born for battle, Mother," Jerylia performed a dramatic, sweeping bow before she led her companions to their usual table just to the right of the royal dais and underneath one of the massive stained glass windows depicting Serra, protector of the throne, and her two sisters: Asayda, goddess of the land who brought them bountiful harvests and formed their snowy peaks with a sweep of her hand and Eowessa, patron of the people who blessed the mountain elves with nature magic.

"You and I need to have a conversation about you laughing while people hold pointy objects to your throat." Adridia addressed the princess as they swung their muscled legs over the wooden bench. "It's happened way too many times when it shouldn't be happening at all."

"I knew you guys could handle it. If anything it's a compliment towards your abilities." She folded her hands neatly in front of her. "You're welcome." She turned towards the warrior sitting next to her.

"Great trick with the ale, Adridia. I don't think I'll ever get used to that." Jerylia wrapped her fingers around the tin cup that was placed in front of her by a servant.

"You're avoiding the topic because you know we're right," Gwera said as she tore apart her dinner roll. Adridia cringed as the witch soaked it in gravy before bringing it to her mouth. "You don't have any powers to fall back on like we do."

"My twenty-sixth birthday is in a month and then my powers will start to appear. Even if I'm half as powerful as my mother, you guys still won't have to worry about me." The table fell into silence. The Queens of Serradon always possessed the same power and they were especially powerful, being descended from the goddess of life herself. They always had control over plant life and even some animal species. The queen had once described it as listening to the song the earth sings and being able to sing along with the notes. Adridia almost understood what that was like. Water had its own voice, always melodic but sometimes tumultuous.

"What's it like?" Jerylia asked, her voice quiet, ocean blue eyes filled with curiosity.

"Shifting powers come on very suddenly. Faryn and I just woke up one morning as eagles. Our parents nearly shit themselves." Theal smiled as he spoke of his ability. The twins were very proud of their shifting powers, a very rare ability, even among mountain elves, which made them extremely valuable to both Jerylia and witches with sinister intentions. Shifter blood and saliva are very valuable ingredients in most fast healing potions so the twins spent a couple of hours in the witch's tower donating both once a month.

"I didn't even realize I had powers until my thirties. My mother was a forest elf and they don't usually possess magical abilities, and if they do it's very little compared to the mountain elves. It wasn't until I began my training as a witch that I realized I had a special connection to the magic in the air," Gwera explained. She had told Adridia the day they met why she was more powerful than other witches but the warrior had no idea she didn't feel her powers at first.

"Your powers will most likely be most similar to mine. We'll both exercise control over something, me: water, and you: plants. It'll come in short bursts at first, brought on by strong emotions. You won't be able to control it until it becomes bigger. Probably closer to your twenty-seventh birthday." Adridia scratched old language symbols into the table with the tip of her dagger as she spoke. "That is why you need to listen to us when we tell you not to laugh in the faces of deadly criminals."

"I may not have my powers yet but I do have you guys and you're more reliable than anything I could ever control." She gave her companions a warm smile.

"Does your father have any powers?" Faryn asked the princess, resting his elbows on the table. The royal consort didn't spend much time in court and he usually only spoke to the queen and his daughter during public events. He was a blacksmith through and through, preferring the solace of his workshop to the machinations of royal life. But he loved his wife and rather than ignore the fact that he was indeed a royal, he had accepted it and chosen to participate even though it made him uncomfortable. Adridia had always admired him for that, especially since she refused to acknowledge her own romantic feelings for the sake of comfort.

"He's a forest elf but dark elf blood runs in his veins, from somewhere very far back." Dark elves had very unnatural abilities, usually something to do with death or the sun, due to their originating in the desert. "He has very weak control over fire. He can make it burn hotter or bigger but not by much and it tires him out so much he doesn't usually bother," the princess explained.

"Your mother married for love, didn't she?" Gwera whispered. They all glanced at the royal table where the queen was laughing with the consort, her eyes sparkling. It wasn't something they talked about much, since Jerylia firmly believed love was something she didn't need, but the way she kept glancing at Kaed from across the room told Adridia that she might have opened herself up to the idea a little bit more.

"She did, fought with my grandmother for years about it. My father is almost three hundred years older than her and my grandmother didn't like the idea of my mother marrying someone that old. But eventually, she gave in, especially when my mother threatened to refuse a mating bond with anyone else, thus ending the royal line. Most elves marry for love. It's sacred." The princess' words were tight as she brought her cup to her lips.

"Yes, but you also have to be mated to someone in order to have a child together," Theal commented. Jerylia frowned.

"This is an unusually serious topic of conversation tonight," she said, looking down at her drink as if she could escape into it.

"Your Highness." The princess looked up when a new voice was added to their group. Kaed Torra, the prince from Torith, stood over their table. "I would request a night stroll through the gardens with you." He flashed her a smile, one that made Adridia bristle. She didn't trust any of the princes vying for Jerylia's hand.

"I accept, but my guard must accompany us." The princess motioned to Adridia. The prince snorted.

"I have no doubt you could face any enemy that dares attack you, but if you insist." He held out a hand to help her off the bench. She waved him off and stood, swinging her leg over. His cheeks flushed a little at the rebuff and Adridia smirked. If he thought Jerylia's heart would be easy to win, he had much to learn. The warrior stood, following the pair out of the warm hall to the chilled gardens, where their breath became visible as it left their mouths. There wasn't much to look at during this time of the year, besides the red snow flowers that seemed to bloom whenever they felt like it.

"I have to admit I wasn't very keen on the idea of marrying so young. I have hundreds of years to live, why live them tethered to someone else?" Adridia could still hear their conversation, which meant she was too close. The warrior had no interest in marriage or mating, but as she watched the princess heir and the foreign prince travel through the bare gardens, arm in arm, a yearning bloomed in her chest. She found herself imagining a marriage and mateship. She ran her fingers over the deep red petals of the snow flowers in bloom, periodically glancing up to ensure the princess was still breathing.

The princess shivered and the prince wrapped his arm around her. Adridia shook her head as she smiled to herself. Jerylia never shivered when she was cold. Gwera must have told her to do that. They stopped near a frozen fountain and turned towards one another. Adridia looked away as the prince bent his head down to kiss Jerylia.

"It's kind of hard to protect me when you can't see me." The warrior turned to find the princess behind her with the prince nowhere in sight. "I sent Kaed along to bed. I didn't want Faryn to miss out on telling them all goodnight." She linked her arm with Adridia's and they began making their way back inside the castle.

"You're being cruel now," the blonde said, although she couldn't hide her smile.

"He's cruel for making us listen to his tales of the bedroom all these years, in explicit detail." The princess countered.

"You forget that not all of those tales happened in the bedroom. Most of them didn't." The girls laughed. They walked in silence a little longer, until they reached the door to the princess heir's rooms.

"Want to come in for a while? It's been a while since we played darts." The warrior gave in and followed the princess to her game room.

"How are you feeling about the princes now?" Adridia asked as she picked up the blue-feathered darts.

"I'm not fond of the other two. The prince from Fastille I'm indifferent about but the one from Saeroc makes me feel slimy. He's handsome, sure, but I have no illusions about what our marriage would be like." She launched her dart at the board, growling in frustration when it stuck near the edge of the circle. "But Kaed, he's kind and handsome and he doesn't mind that I've killed more men than years I've lived, Adri."

"I don't like any of them. I hate the idea of you marrying a stranger, Jer." The warrior took her turn, launching her darts at the wooden board. Adridia understood why Jerylia didn't want to marry Faryn but she never gave him a chance and she had listened to him speak about her endlessly. She didn't know why she was pushing so hard for it. Maybe Jerylia was right and she was transferring her feelings for Theal onto Faryn and the princess.

"I know you think I should be with Faryn, but there's too much history there. I value his friendship too much. Plus, I hate how boastful he is about his conquests. I will always wonder if I am just another notch on his bow. I could never see him as anything more than a brother in arms." She shrugged her shoulders. Adridia clenched her jaw before sighing in defeat. She knew once Jerylia made up her mind there was no changing it and she didn't want to fight with her again.

"I know. You have my blessing," Jerylia snorted.

"I didn't need your blessing."

"Maybe not officially, but deep down you knew you needed it."

"No, I was pretty much going to do it anyway. Besides, you sorta gave me your blessing when you said he could throw me up against a wall."

"Oh, yeah, I did say that."

"That reminds me, I need you to teach me how to be good at all that stuff before my wedding night."

"With men, it's really not that hard. As long as you've got tits and an ass, they'll have no problem finishing."

"Still, I need some help. Faryn and Theal are no help about it."

"Then class is in session, and you had better take notes."

"Yes, ma'am." They both laughed to each other, the darts game forgotten.

Chapter 4

Jerylia

"Queen Aselidda. Mother." The princess stood before her mother's throne, the prince from Torith just a few feet behind her. "I stand before you to announce my immediate engagement to Prince Kaed Torra of Torith." The princess reached behind her to intertwine fingers with the prince and pull him forward so he was standing next to her. The queen smiled broadly at her daughter.

"That is wonderful news. We'll host the wedding on your birthday and all of the foreign royals will be in attendance." Aselidda stood and descended the steps to envelop her daughter in a hug. "I am happy you found love, my heart," she whispered in Jerylia's ear. The princess just gave her a weak smile. "We have only three weeks to plan a royal wedding but it should be just enough. I want you trying on gowns this afternoon and cake tasting tomorrow."

"I didn't realize I had to help plan it." Jerylia had planned to escape the duties of planning her wedding.

"Well, I'm not doing it by myself, it's torture enough as it is. I know you would rather be scouting out your next mission for your squadron, but this event is a necessity. A royal wedding is a rare event but one that keeps the people in high spirits." The queen planted a soft kiss on her daughter's forehead. "I promise you'll have plenty of time for adventuring. I'm planning on living a long time yet." She gave a wink before leaving the couple alone in the throne room.

"Are you sure I'm the one you want to marry?" Kaed folded Jerylia's hands in his own, looking her in the eye. She smiled up at him.

"Kaed, I know we've only known each other a week but when I look at you, everything slows down. It's just you and me in the room. I know eight hundred years is a long time and sometimes I can be a difficult person to live with, but if you'll have me, I'll have you. Plus you make a pretty good sparring partner." She stood on her toes to kiss him quickly, his smile forming that blasted dimple in his cheek. Gods, he would be the death of her. "Are you sure you're okay just being a consort? I mean you were in line to be King of Torith."

"My parents have been telling me for a long time that I might not be the one to lead Torith. They taught me that it was a greater honor to be chosen by a descendant of an actual goddess than it is to be king." He grinned and looked her up and down. "Although, looking at you, I'm beginning to think I was chosen by a goddess herself." The princess laughed loudly and allowed him to pull her to his chest, capturing her lips in a breath-taking kiss. Their flirtation was intoxicating and Jerylia could feel something swelling in her chest, warmth spreading through her body. She wrapped her arms around his neck and his hands flew to her hips, squeezing tight, drawing the entire length of her body flush against his. She pulled her mouth from his and smiled up at him.

"Keep using lines like that and you'll get a whole lot more from me."

"Well, I know if you were a chicken, you'd be impeccable." Her body shook as laughter wracked through her and suddenly he was the only thing holding her up.

"That was a good one," she said once the laughter had ceased. He was smiling, perfect teeth flashing. He kissed her again, this one more breathless than the last. His hands slid down to her thighs and he hoisted her up, wrapping her legs around his hips as his feet moved across the floor. The stone wall was cold against her back as she collided with it. Her fingers threaded through his hair and he separated from her mouth to trail kisses down her neck, sweeping her hair out of the way. She closed her eyes against the pleasure sweeping over her skin. "Kaed," she whispered, tugging his hair slightly. He returned to her mouth, giving her two quick kisses before pulling away completely, though she was still propped up against the wall. He moved to let her down but she stopped him with a hand on his arm. "Hold on, I need a minute for my legs to work."

"I apologize, Frumoasa."

"What does that mean?" Her mother had forced her to learn the languages of the other countries, so she was fluent in all six known languages but she wanted to hear him say it in Serradonian. He smiled warmly at her.

"I know you speak Torithian, Princess."

"Say it anyway." He leaned his forehead against hers.

"Beautiful," he whispered before capturing her lips once again. Gods, he was intoxicating. She couldn't get enough of him. A loud cough caught their attention and they ripped apart to see Gwera a few feet away with her arms folded over her chest.

"Whenever you two are done, Jerylia, your mother has some gowns for you to try on."

"Already?" Kaed let her down but kept a firm hand on her waist for support in case her legs gave in.

"She works fast." Gwera strode forward and placed her hands on Jerylia's cheeks, turning her head to the side. "And now

I need to tell her to get one with a high collar." Jerylia blushed and glared at Kaed who had the nerve to look sheepish.

"They'll be gone by the wedding and I guess Kaed will just have to keep his hands off of me." She separated herself from him and followed Gwera out of the throne room. She glanced over her shoulder to see her prince gazing at the sway of her hips.

"You are cruel, Princess." She only grinned at him, sending a wink before the thick doors closed behind her. Gwera eyed her carefully.

"You're smitten," she commented.

"Maybe I am. He makes me feel good in every sort of way. I know I was adamant about not getting married but this might not be so bad." Her mind was already wandering back to her prince and the way she felt when he kissed her, when his hands gripped her hips like she were a lifeline, when his lips pressed against her neck. She found herself waiting for the time to pass so she could fold herself into his arms again. He made her feel like it was okay to be vulnerable when she hadn't been for so long and, yet, he also appreciated the warrior in her and admired that side of her. She had never felt this way about anyone and the thought of him brought a content smile to her lips.

The next three weeks passed in a blur of wedding planning and stolen kisses when no one was around. Her companions teased her endlessly about her change in demeanor but she didn't mind. She liked that Kaed was the one to bring about this change in her and for all their teasing, they liked him. He ate meals with the five of them, saying he wanted to get to know Jerylia's four closest friends. Jerylia's heart was full and she knew she had reached her peak happiness but there was a feeling tugging at her gut, that something was about to go wrong. Something was about to happen and she couldn't shake the dread she felt.

The night before her wedding, the princess ate dinner alone in her rooms. She didn't want her companions or her fiancé to see the way her hands shook. She was startled by a knock on the thick wooden door. She sighed, exhausted from wedding rehearsals that had taken up the majority of her day. She stood, her wet hair dripping on the marble floors as she strode to open the door. "Oh, it's you." She turned back around and took her seat at the table once again. "I hope you don't mind if I finish my dinner. I'm exhausted."

"Then I'll try to make this quick." Faryn sat down in the chair next to her, turning it so he could face her. "I know Adridia told you about my feelings for you." Jerylia stood abruptly, her chair scraping on the floor.

"I guess I'm not hungry anymore." She tossed her napkin on her half-empty plate before stalking into the adjoining room that housed her massive bed.

"Please just hear me out." He grabbed her wrists and forced her to face him.

"I can't because I am getting married tomorrow, Faryn. No matter what, I am getting married tomorrow. I have to for the sake of my kingdom." She looked at the floor, anger flaring in her chest.

"I love you, Jerylia." She ripped her arms from his hands and sat on the edge of her bed, refusing to meet his eyes, to acknowledge the pain she knew would buckle her resolve. He knelt in front of her so he could look her in the eye, the love and pain in their depths nearly knocking her over. She clenched her jaw and turned her head. "I know you think I sleep around too much and that I wouldn't be a faithful husband, but the only reason I sought solace in other women was that I knew you wouldn't have me and it was tearing me apart." She was silent, a frown on her mouth. Of course, he would blame her rather than accept that this was just who he was: a whore who used women and then tossed them aside once their time was done. Theal was the same way and yet she had never been disgusted about the way he or Adridia went about their sexual endeavors. Maybe it was because they always spoke about past lovers with respect whereas Faryn treated it like a game, something to gossip about. It sickened her to think of herself as one of those women he would brag about finally bedding.

"So you would use my rejection as an excuse for the horrible way you treat women. I am getting *married* tomorrow. If you really loved me you should have said something sooner, instead, I had to hear it from Adridia." Her voice was sharp but her chest ached. She didn't love him in the same way he loved her. So she had to push him away. "You don't love me, Faryn. You only love the idea of having the one elf that you can't."

"Marry me instead." His eyes were pleading.

"And risk a war with Torith? We've been at peace for thousands of years and you want me to risk that because you have a crush?" She stood and strode to her window, looking up at the night sky. "I need you to leave, Faryn. I've allowed you to entertain this idea for too long and now it's time to stop." She whirled around to face him, fire in her eyes. "I am not the one for you. I won't make you happy. I know you think this is love but you have no idea what love is. If we were meant to be, then I would return your feelings but I don't. So leave me alone." Her voice had gotten deathly quiet with her final words. The archer squared his shoulders back, a mask coming over his features.

"Then forget this ever happened, your highness." His words dripped with venom. "Congratulations on your wedding tomorrow." He turned and ducked out the door, leaving her to slump against the window ledge. Her chest shook as tears ran down her face. She didn't even glance up as a tall figure emerged from her bathroom.

"You told me he would try to stop the wedding." The princess had stopped crying and now rested her head against the glass window.

"That was hard to hear. I didn't think he would be so adamant." Adridia approached her friend.

"Gods, I can't believe him. Coming here hoping I would do what? Cancel my wedding for him? Not only do I have an entire kingdom waiting and relying on my marriage, but the other royals have been here for a month to attend my wedding. He can't just come here and make these demands of me because he thinks I owe him something." Anger was flowing through her as Adridia pulled her into a tight hug.

"I'm sorry that I ever tried to convince you to marry him. I've seen you with Kaed and it's so obvious that you two belong together." She pulled away, concern in her eyes. "You're shaking like a hairless rabbit, what's wrong?"

"I was already shaking because of nerves for the wedding and I've had this feeling for weeks now that something bad is coming and I can't shake it and now Faryn and everything and I just can't breathe." Her breath was being stolen from her lungs and she couldn't quite catch it. Adridia pulled her into another embrace, squeezing her tight until the panic passed. "Thank you, Adri."

"I think you should go tell your prince that you love him. It might soothe your nerves about tomorrow." Jerylia nodded, wiping the tears from her cheeks. She did feel very strongly about Kaed. Maybe it wasn't quite love yet but there was always time for that after the wedding. She wanted him to know before they stood together at the altar that this was how she felt and would continue to feel. That nagging feeling only pushed her to do it more. If something bad was coming, she wanted him to know. She left Adridia in her bedroom and ran to the hall that housed the royals from Torith. Kaed looked surprised to see her at his door.

"Dragul Meu, what are you doing here, this is bad luck." Her heart melted at the Torithian term for 'my love'.

"I have to tell you something."

"Now?" She nodded and he welcomed her into his room.

"I'm nervous about tomorrow and I mean, it's my wedding, and the entire kingdom is attending and expecting great things of me, and what if I can't live up to their expectations? But I can't shake the feeling that I'm going fuck something up and just because I love you doesn't mean that the marriage will work, what if something goes wrong and I can't handle being the queen and being a wife and I have too many labels on me and I just need to-" He cut her off with a kiss. She relaxed into his arms and he pulled away.

"You love me?" Her cheeks burned.

"Um, yeah. I do and I wanted to tell you before we were bound to each other forever." He grinned and kissed her again.

"I love you too." His lips met hers and she melted into him. They spent the night wrapped up in each other before falling asleep tangled in each other's arms.

Jerylia jerked awake as the twin moons were just beginning to disappear over the mountain peaks. She sat up and gazed down at her prince, so peaceful. He had understood the night before when she could only promise him kisses and nothing more. She leaned down and pressed a kiss to his temple. He groaned and his eyes slid open.

"I have to go, but I'll see you later." He smiled and leaned up for a kiss. "I love you," he whispered against her lips. She smiled and returned the sentiment before slipping out of his bed and sneaking back to her room.

Jerylia spent the morning being prepared, her hair being tugged in every direction and her face being pinched to force redness into her cheeks. Her handmaidens forced her into a white dress that hugged her body and belled out at her hips. Sheer sleeves wrapped around her arms, white threads of ivy embroidered into the sleeves and skirt, climbing up to the bodice. Her hair was wrapped around her head in a braided crown, loose strands pulled out to frame her face, with snow flowers stuck into the braid to bring some color to the ensemble.

"I don't envy you in the slightest," Adridia said from where she leaned against the doorway. Jerylia gave her an obscene gesture which made her handmaidens gasp and swat at her hands.

"I should have forced you to wear a dress as well," she muttered under her breath. The queen had declared the wedding a formal event so the warrior was wearing a split skirt over leggings and had been forced into an armored corset over her red shirt.

"I'm suffering enough in this contraption. I can hardly breathe." She pressed a hand to her stomach.

"I have to admit, I don't hate this dress." The princess ran her hand over the folds of white chiffon around her.

"I still can't believe you're not wearing armor," Adridia commented.

"Kaed requested to see me in something other than armor or leggings for once," she snorted. "He had better cherish this because it won't ever be happening again."

"It's nearly time, princess." The head handmaiden brought in a cherry wood box. She tipped open the lid to reveal a delicate crown that matched her mother's wreath of silver ivy. She nestled the crown in Jerylia's thick hair. "You are ready. We'll take our leave. Your mother should be here soon to escort you to the throne room." The handmaidens left, Adridia followed after wishing the princess all the luck in the world.

Left alone, the princess pressed a hand to her stomach as she looked herself over. She looked more regal than ever with her hair piled on her head, leaving the column of her neck exposed and a crown nestled into the thick locks, sparkling in the sunlight streaming through her window. The starkness of some of her tattoos stood out against her pale skin, a smoking sword visible on her forearm and hints of a wolf etched across her back. Butterflies fluttered in her chest, nervousness settling over her. A sharp gasp had her turning towards the door. Her mother had tears in her eyes, her hand covering her mouth.

"You look like a queen, my heart." She took her daughter's hands in her own. Jerylia looked down, noticing for the first time, wrinkles beginning to appear there. She had never thought of her mother as old but as she studied her, for the first time in years, she saw signs of age beginning to appear. The queen would live for centuries yet, but Jerylia would take over as queen long before her mother joined the goddesses.

"I feel like one, for the first time. I feel like this is what I was born for." The princess blinked away tears.

"Shall we?" The queen looped her elbow through her daughter's and led her through the castle.

"Her royal majesty, Queen Aselidda Dwymeth Serra, escorting her first and only born daughter, Princess Jerylia Dwymeth Serra." They heard the announcer just before the doors opened to allow them through. Half the kingdom had been packed into the room and they all looked at her. She was not new to being the center of attention and squared her shoulders, her head held high as she strode down the aisle. She caught the eye of her prince, Kaed and he smiled at her. She returned it, eagerly.

She ducked as a roar shook the castle and rubble began falling from the ceiling. A dark shadow fell over the room and a massive black dragon landed in front of them, a dark figure on its back.

Chapter 5

Gwera

Gwera twisted her fingers, forming the movements with her hands to cast the only spell that might allow her to save the princess. She held her palms vertically, placing them together for the final movement before separating them swiftly. Everything in the room stopped moving. She only had a few minutes to grab the princess and get her out. The rest of her companions were still able to move and aided her in collecting the princess. She glanced back at the queen, who lay on the floor, blood dripping from her head wound. There wasn't time. The witch bit down on her resolve and dragged the princess through a side door, cloaking the door so no one would come after them. Time resumed and every sound from the great hall could be heard from where they hid. The princess was barely conscious, blood seeping from a small wound on her temple. Gwera grabbed Theal's tunic and pulled his face down so he was level with her. She stuck a finger in his mouth, collecting his saliva before letting him go. He made a disgusted face and wiped at his lips while she spread his spit over Jerylia's head wound, whispering the words to a simple healing spell.

"Bring them all to the front! I want to look down on them," a woman growled, most likely the woman who had been riding the huge black dragon that had collapsed the ceiling. She laughed, the sound almost musical, and Jerylia began to stir, her eyes fluttering open. Gwera covered her mouth and motioned for her to be quiet. "Queen Aselidda," the voice drawled.

"You don't know what you've done, Princess." They heard the queen snarl, ever the warrior.

"Oh, you haven't heard?" The voice was smooth, beautiful almost yet filled with poison, like an emerald snake. "It's Empress now," she purred. "Allow me to demonstrate the power I wield." The room became silent. "Kill the princes." Jerylia's eyes widened before they heard multiple sickening squelching sounds followed by wet thuds. The princess closed her eyes as tears slid over her cheeks. Her companions bowed their heads in honor of the fallen royals.

"So not only have you declared war on Serradon, but you're risking war on the others as well?" The queen was clearly struggling against some sort of restraint.

"That's actually the whole plan. I loved my mother dearly but she never saw what Draerige could truly be. She never thought that we could easily conquer all of Cordava. Draerige is the biggest country, not by much, mind you, but we still take that crown. And we are the only country that hosts dragons." As if to punctuate her sentence a deep growl resonated throughout the room. There was a moment of silence, filled only by the sound of footsteps, slow and determined. "Where is the blushing bride, by the way?" the empress asked.

"Hopefully somewhere you'll never find her," the queen hissed. They heard the sound of a sword unsheathing followed by a guttural shout. They heard the distinct sound of a knife sinking into a soft stomach.

"Nice try, consort," the empress whispered.

"Goodbye, my love." They heard the queen's consort whisper before they heard his final breath. Jerylia writhed in

Adridia's arms. The warrior brought her hand up to cover the princess' mouth and Gwera removed hers, probing the cloak over the door with her magic to make sure no sound could escape.

"You have to be quiet," Gwera whispered.

"Your mother was not weak. She was a great leader. There were many things we didn't agree on but that never curbed my admiration of her," they heard the queen say through clenched teeth.

"You are a monster," she almost growled. The castle walls shuddered around them, green vines creeping through the bricks.

"Knock her out, now!" they heard the empress shout. The rumbling stopped and they heard a body slump to the floor. "I want every inch of this palace searched now! We must find the princess! I have a special blade I want to use to remove her head." They heard the empress shout, a violent sort of glee edged her voice.

"We have to go, now," Gwera whispered to her companions. Jerylia's eyes widened and she struggled against Adridia, her head shaking. "I know you don't want to leave your mother but if we don't leave the empress will find you and she will kill you without hesitation. You are your mother's best hope for a rescue." The witch tried to reason with her princess.

"I can't hold her much longer, Gwera." Adridia clenched her jaw and the muscles in her arms bulged, veins popping through as Jerylia fought against her hold.

"I'm sorry, Jer," Gwera whispered, resting her palm on the heir's forehead. The witch whispered a few words before Jerylia's eyes flashed green and her body slumped in the warrior's arms. "Faryn, help carry her. Theal, scout ahead."

The twins nodded and they began moving through the narrow hallways that the servants used. They eventually reached the kitchens where they could access the tunnels underneath the castle. The tunnels emptied out in the sewers that ran underneath the streets of the Serramor.

"Disgusting." Faryn gagged at the smell of waste.

"Well, would you rather be in the belly of a dragon?" Adridia hissed at him, straining to keep Jerylia's head above the shit-water.

"Do you want me to answer that honestly? Cause that sounds better than looking at your ugly mug," Faryn jeered at her.

"If I wasn't carrying my best friend through sewer water, you would so have a dagger through the eye right now," the warrior threatened.

"Yes, but you are, so I don't," he countered.

"Can you two stop fighting for ten minutes, please?" Theal grumbled from up front. The group came to a set of stairs leading to a small circular hole covered by a thick slab of wood. The archer shoved his shoulder against it to move it to the side. "Gwera, can you cloak us?"

The witch nodded and closed her eyes for a moment, her fingers bending unnaturally as she performed the movements for a more elaborate cloaking spell. She could feel the exhaustion seeping into her body. She didn't know how much longer she would be able to keep her eyes open. The magic in the air was powerful and her special connection to it made her more powerful than any other witch in the kingdom but drawing on it used up her energy and the time-stopping spell had used up so much of it. Her eyes snapped open after a moment and she nodded sharply, concentration creasing her brow as she kept one palm facing straight up and the other sideways and perpendicular to it, holding the spell in place.

"We just have to make it to the edge of the city. My father

will have a mount and a cart we can borrow." They all nodded at each other before stepping out of the sewers. The capital city was in chaos. Dragons flew overhead, the streets shaking from the force of their roars. Serradonians were everywhere, screaming as they ran for cover. The five companions crept through the back alleys. A small child sat in the middle of a street, crying. Adridia scooped her up, Gwera allowing the cloak to slip from her for a moment. The warrior delivered the child to her home and Gwera prayed that her parents were still alive. They finally reached Adridia's childhood home and slipped inside. The witch released her hold on the cloak, exhaustion settling over her bones.

"Addie, what are you doing here?" Adridia rolled her eyes at the nickname but greeted her father with a tight embrace.

"We need a horse and a cart, father. We need to get the princess out of the capital, out of Serradon if we must." The warrior was frantic. Ward Ibyr nodded, his eyes shifting to the rest of her companions.

"Stay here, pack some food for the journey. I'll go get the cart ready. You'll be taking Ivy with you." The elder Ibyr stood but Adridia stopped him with a hand covering his.

"I can't take Ivy. She's your most reliable mount."

Her father gave her a soft smile. "That is precisely why I am sending her with you." He gave her no room for argument as he left the sizable cottage.

"Where are we going to go, Adri?" Gwera asked the warrior.

"Fraton is the closest village to here. Sinisstra won't risk venturing into the mountains, not yet. She's not familiar with the terrain and neither are her dragons. We'll go there and wait for Jerylia to wake and figure out what we are going to do next." They all looked at the snoozing princess who had been laid down on the wooden bench near the hearth. Gwera's heart softened as she gazed at her princess. She was going to wake and she would remember the trail of death that had brought them here, to this exact moment. Her father was gone and had used his last breath to tell the queen he loved her. Her prince had been killed as a show of power and Jerylia hadn't even gotten to say goodbye. Gwera's heart broke for the young elf. She was only twenty-six, too young to experience this kind of violence and heartbreak.

"It's her birthday and her home was invaded," she said softly, combing Jerylia's caramel hair away from her face.

"We need to get her out of that ridiculous dress," Faryn grumbled, his arms folded over his chest.

"I have some clothes here from when I was younger that she can wear. It might be a tight squeeze but they'll do the job until we can buy some for her. You two go help my father." Adridia pushed the twin archers out the door before she disappeared up the wooden staircase. She reappeared a few moments later with a wine-colored cotton shirt and a pair of brown trousers. The two women struggled to get the princess both out of her wedding dress and into the clothes.

"What do we do with the dress?" Adridia gathered it into her arms.

"I'll store it in my old bedroom. Maybe we can come back for it sometime in the future." The warrior disappeared back up the stairs before returning with a thin breastplate and some arm coverings. "Can you help me out of this corset? Jerylia can wear it so at least she has some protection. I can wear this." Gwera set to work unlacing the black corset and wrapped it around the princess, lacing it back up almost expertly, careful not to make it too tight so she could breathe.

"We're ready." Faryn burst into the cottage, a sheen of sweat covering his forehead. Together, they hoisted the princess up, grunting with effort. "Remind me to tell her to lay off the ale when she wakes up."

"And the potatoes, holy goddesses," Adridia grunted.

"You two forget that she's mostly muscle." Gwera chastised. "And she's self-conscious about her weight so shut up." They managed to get her settled in the back of the horse cart, throwing a blanket over her to keep her warm in the chilled mountain air. Gwera sat next to her and positioned Jerylia's head in her lap in case she woke up.

"Goodbye, my dear. Protect our princess at all costs. She is our only hope, as are you." Ward Ibyr gripped his daughter's hand as they said their goodbyes. Gwera swallowed and looked away from the father and daughter, bitterness filling her stomach. Adridia took her place at the front of the cart and after a swift snap of the reins, the cart lurched forward. Gwera looked back at the capital, her home for so many years and one silent tear trailed down her cheek.

Chapter 6

Jerylia

The princess woke with a splitting headache. She brought a hand to her forehead as she sat up in the bed she had been laid in. She looked down at herself. Someone had dressed her in a dark green cotton shirt with a wide neck that exposed her collarbones under the same armored corset Adridia had worn to her wedding and a pair of tight black pants. The wolf pommel of her treasured sword gleamed in the candlelight from where it sat propped against the bed frame. She grabbed it and laid it across her lap, her fingers running over the scabbard. The matching dagger rested on a table that sat next to the bed. She leaned back against the wall, running a hand through her now unbound hair as she fought the tears that sprang forward as memories bombarded her. Her father was dead. Her prince was dead. Her mother was a prisoner. Her kingdom was invaded and she didn't even know where she was. Gods, what a mess.

"Oh good, you're finally awake." The princess looked up as Adridia entered the small room.

"Where are we? The last thing I remember is—" The princess shut her eyes against the painful memories.

"Gwera had to knock you out so we could get you out of the capital. We borrowed a cart from my father and came here to Fraton." The warrior explained from the doorway. "Come downstairs and have dinner with us. We'll explain the plan." The warrior turned and went back out the only door in the room. The princess sighed and stood, strapping her sword around her waist and her dagger around her thigh before tucking her feet into the pair of worn black leather boots sitting next to the bed.

The tavern was busy but her friends had managed to secure a booth in the back corner. They all had full plates in front of them and, despite the cheery atmosphere of the tavern, all wore grim faces.

"She lives." Faryn held up his cup and nodded to her before he took a long drink from it. All of her companions wore sad smiles, all masking their exhaustion.

"I am beyond angry at all of you but acting on that rage is not going to be beneficial for us right now," she stated calmly as she slid into the booth.

"If I hadn't done what I did, we would probably all be dead right now. She needs your mother alive but she has no need for you. She said something about a blade she picked out just to remove your head," Gwera leaned forward and whispered. She eyed the princess' long hair. "You should cut or dye your hair." The princess gasped and grabbed the thick curls defensively.

"I should smack you for even suggesting it." Jerylia flicked her hair behind her back.

"Queens are required to wear their hair long," she stated proudly.

"Then you need to wear it up. Your hair is very recognizable." The witch stated, stabbing her cooked potatoes with a bent fork. Jerylia frowned, plucking the leather strip from Theal's wrist. She tied her hair into a large knot on her head before beginning on her own dinner in front of her.

"He's here," Gwera whispered to the small group, her eyes pinned on the doorway.

The princess turned to see a middle-aged male elf enter the tavern.

"Who is he?" she asked her companions.

"Just watch. You'll want to see this." The man set up a stool on a small stage in the opposite corner of the tavern. He pulled a stringed instrument out of the case he had been carrying and set it on one leg, plucking the strings delicately.

"I'm going to tell you a tale, a tale of dragons and glory." Jerylia quickly realized the man was not going to sing, much to her disappointment, but as he started speaking, small illusions appeared in front of him. She had heard of performers with illusion magic but had never been lucky enough to see one for herself. Her curiosity was piqued as she leaned forward and rested her elbows on her knees to see him better. "Far to the east, there stands an island country, called Hrinth, where dragons terrorized elves of all shapes and sizes. They are governed by the goddess Della, who saw her people's terror and fear and sought a way to aid them. She searched far and wide, even contacting the other gods for help in her search. She brought her troubles to the triplet goddess, begging them for help. Serra didn't trust Della and was going to refuse but Eowessa felt Della's compassion for her people, a compassion they shared. She convinced her sisters to allow Della to choose one of their people, a Serradonian who would grow to resolve their dragon problem in exchange for Della allowing Asayda to choose one of her own people in return for any future issues that may arise. Della took the deal, desperate to help her people. That is how the dragonslayer was chosen.

"There was an elf born in Serradon with mountain blood who exhibited no signs of power once his twenty-sixth year came around. He was disgraced by his family. A mountain elf who shows no sign of power is known as a Shorr, a defect, a stain that doesn't belong. It is believed they are bad luck to house and home because their blood is defective. So he was cast out, unwanted. He journeyed all over Cordava, seeking out a place he wanted to call home. Eventually, he journeyed over the sea, towards the call he felt in the distance, pulling him towards Hrinth. He arrived on that island country and felt everything. He was Della's chosen and he had a unique power, one that was no use to him in Serradon. He could speak to the dragons and calm them. Some stories even say he could turn into one. He used this power of his to lure the dragons and slay them, one by one until the dragons could no longer terrorize the people of Hrinth.

"When he was done with his task, he looked at himself and couldn't bear what he saw. He was shamed by how he had used his gods-given powers, how he had used them to slay such beautiful creatures. He fled to the north, to the abandoned mountainous region where he now lives in self-assigned exile, in shame, forever alone until he learns to accept what he did." Jerylia turned back around to face the table once the storyteller was finished.

"So what, you want to go find this dragonslayer? For what purpose? We know how to kill a dragon, stab it with the pointy end of your sword," Jerylia quipped.

"It's not that simple. Eventually, you would kill a dragon that way but it would take a long time due to their thick skin. This dragonslayer may be our only chance at gaining the upper hand." The princess turned to see the performer settle into a corner booth with a single mug in front of him.

"I'm going to go talk to him." The princess rose, her sword shifting with her. Theal stood with her.

"I'll join you." Jerylia flared her nostrils once in slight annoyance before approaching the performer's booth.

"Good evening," the princess greeted. The performer smiled up at them.

"You look rather inquisitive, princess. Please, won't you join me?" Jerylia hid her shock well, sliding into the booth smoothly. "My name is Civ. What would you like to know?"

"Was your story true?" she asked, her voice low.

"Honestly I have no idea. I'd like to believe it's true as I heard it first-hand from one of my brother's shipmates, he's from Hrinth and claimed to have lived through the blight himself. Said it happened only a hundred and fifty years ago and the dragonslayer was quite young, still is, compared to me." It's true, elves were considered young until they were at least two centuries old.

"Do you know where to find the dragonslayer?" the princess asked.

"All I know is that he is known as the dragonslayer. You could go to Hrinth and ask around, I hear some people know where to find him." The older elf was beginning to frustrate the pair with his cryptic words.

"But how are we supposed to get to Hrinth? The empress probably has her army checking every passenger ship that departs looking for me." Her hand formed a fist on the table. "And I can't exactly abandon my country during all of this."

"Maybe we should go. It gets you out of danger and we could look for this dragonslayer. He could turn the tide of this war," Theal reasoned.

"Go to Shemon. My brother owns a ship, calls it 'The Lady Fair'. Tell him Civ sent you. He'll get you where you need to go." The elf took a long drink from his cup.

"What if he doesn't believe us?" Theal asked, always the inquisitive one, foreseeing problems that the rest of them might not.

"I love my brother but Peld doesn't make his money doin' honest work. He'll most likely be smuggling something, probably snow flowers. The Hrinthians grind 'em up and use them to make a very potent drug mostly used in brothels. Blackmail him into giving you passage." The princess and her companion nodded and slid out of the booth. "Oh, princess?" Jerylia turned to look at him as he sent her a wink. "Your whereabouts are safe with me." She gave a sigh of relief before flashing a smile.

"Thank you, Civ." He nodded slightly. They returned to their booth, curiosity brimming in their companions' eyes.

"What did he say?" Gwera was the first to ask.

"We'll be heading to Shemon in the morning. His brother is going to give us a ride to Hrinth where we can look for our dragonslayer."

Chapter 7

Faryn

"Do you live here in Fraton?" Faryn flashed a smile at the brunette he was trying to bed at the bar. His mind kept flashing back to that night, the night before Jerylia's wedding. The way she spoke to him, he had never heard that tone in her voice before. He cleared his mind, focusing back on the task before him. She smiled shyly and tucked her hair behind her ear, nodding in answer to his question. He leaned in closer, so he was able to smell the vanilla of her perfume.

"My father owns the dairy farm on the outskirts," she replied. He heard a laugh pierce the rest of the tavern noise. His eyes wandered past the elf in front of him to land on Jerylia. Her head was tipped back as a laugh sprang from her lips. She still had a smile on her face as she took a deep drink of her ale. He was happy she was laughing. She had been devastated when she woke up, but he thought the hope of the dragonslayer had lifted her spirits a bit. His eyes were drawn to her face, to the relaxed expression she wore. Her lips were drawn up in an easy smile and her eyes were hooded from the drink in her hand. Her cheeks were flushed from the heat of the tavern and the drink in her blood. His chest ached the longer he gazed at her from across the bar. He shook his head and brought his attention back to the young maiden in front of him. "He hates it when I come here, but he doesn't know that's exactly why I do it." The girl shifted closer to him, drawing her hair away from her neck.

"Not a daddy's girl?" he asked, his voice low as his gaze shifted once more. The princess was certainly more muscular than the girl in front of him, her body formed by years of practice with a sword, and curvier around her chest and hips from eating well. That gods-damned corset Adridia had given her for armor only accentuated her curves and it was torturing him. A cough in front of him brought his attention back.

"Listen, I'm here for a reason and if you can't fulfil that reason then I need to move on. I have to be back on the farm in the morning." The shy girl he had been speaking to just a moment ago was gone, replaced by a woman who knew exactly what she wanted. He only lifted a brow at her boldness.

"I'm sorry," he apologized before leaving her alone at the bar and re-joining his companions. Which he immediately regretted when he sat down.

"Aw, poor Faryn failed to find a sheath for his sword," Adridia slurred as he leaned back in his chair, drinking deeply from the cup he had brought back from the bar.

"At least I can get laid," he shot back. She sneered at him before leaning her head on Jerylia's shoulder. The princess rested her cheek on the warrior's blonde head.

"It's different for women than it is for men. For us, we are more guaranteed to finish alone than with a partner," Gwera commented, running a finger around the rim of her cup absentmindedly.

"Unless that partner is also female," Adridia pointed out. The warrior was just as successful as the twins at bedding strangers. She'd had many partners over the past few years, elves of all races and genders. She didn't discriminate who would end up tangled in her sheets. "I feel bad that you'll never discover that for yourself." Adridia poked Jerylia's cheek.

"Oh, believe me, I've had experiences with orgasms." Faryn choked on his drink when the princess said that.

"Oh, he chokes," Gwera said dejectedly.

"Can we not talk about my sex life please?" Faryn groaned.

"Maybe if you didn't boast about it so much we wouldn't. We don't mock Theal about it because he doesn't boast about it," Gwera explained.

"I told you your big mouth would eventually get you in trouble, brother," his twin commented, a smile on his lips.

"Believe me, my mouth usually only gets the women in trouble," he punctuated with a wink and a smirk.

"That is exactly the point, Faryn." Gwera pointed at him and he shrugged.

"We should all be going to bed. We have to leave at first light." Jerylia stood. Adridia stood with her and followed her up the stairs to their rented rooms.

"Let's go. I'm going to follow you to make sure you don't get into trouble." Gwera grabbed the twins by their collars and pulled them up. "Come on, off to bed you go." She pushed them up the stairs with a hand on each of their backs.

"Okay, Mother."

Faryn woke to someone pounding on the door of the cramped room. "Haul your asses out of bed, you oafs. We're wasting daylight." Jerylia's voice was muffled through the door.

"I forgot what a joy she is in the morning," Theal grumbled as he rubbed the sleep from his eyes.

"I heard that," Faryn chuckled as his twin froze.

"She's got ears like an eagle, brother," Faryn commented as his twin scowled. They quickly dressed in the questionably dirty clothes they had been wearing the previous day and met the three women in the tavern on the first floor. The princess held a woven basket with various fruits, cheeses, and bread, most likely for their journey to the shore.

"Ivy is ready to go right outside the tavern. We should reach the coast by this afternoon." Adridia adjusted her belt that held her sword. The group of companions was quiet as they left the tavern and burst onto the already busy street. Adridia's beloved horse was already attached to the small cart they had ridden here in. Faryn shivered as fat flakes of snow fell around them, pulling his cloak tighter around himself. Three of the five companions piled onto the small cart, Adridia and Jerylia taking the front to steer the strong horse.

"Wake me up when we get there," Gwera mumbled and curled up, wrapping herself in her cloak.

"It's colder than a snowman's ass out here," Adridia grumbled, pulling her cloak tighter around herself.

"I'm inclined to agree with you," Gwera mumbled from the back of the cart as she looked out over the landscape around them.

"Gwera, snuggle with me, it'll keep us warm." Faryn reached for the small witch who slapped his hands away.

"Touch me, and you'll have blue snot for a year."

"I'll cuddle with you, brother," Theal offered, a smirk set on his lips.

"Pass, but thanks." Theal smiled and shook his head.

"Will you babies please be quiet? We live in Serradon. Ice flows through our veins and steel sings in our ears." Jerylia's cheeks were flushed from the cold and her breath formed clouds in front of her. He heard the pride she had for her kingdom in her words. She had a determined smile set on her lips as she wrapped her arms around herself.

They arrived in Shemon in the early afternoon. Theal and Gwera went in search of a place to stay for the night while the princess, Adridia, and Faryn went in search of The Lady Fair. A few ships were bobbing in the water at the docks. Pulley systems allowed the ship crews to load the cargo onto the ships from the stilted docks that had been built to reach the top decks of the ships. The stilted docks were one of the many wonders that brought people to Serradon. Many merchants preferred to dock here because of the easy loading system and the extra deep marina. Adridia pointed out a ship in the middle of the row with golden letters sparkling in the afternoon sun, painted on the back of the ship. A man that could have been a twin to Civ the performer was barking orders at his shipmates, a wrinkled manifest dangling from his fingers.

"Excuse me." Jerylia marched up to the man, her eyes fierce.

"Can I help ya?" He squinted in the bright sunlight.

"I want to travel to Hrinth on your boat. We met your brother at a tavern in Fraton and he told us you would give us safe passage."

The man scoffed at her. "I don't know what my brother told you, but my ship is no place for civilians." He looked them up and down, taking in their tattoos and weapons. "Even if you are well versed in battle. Now if you'll excuse me, I was in the middle of something." He turned to walk away. Jerylia visibly bristled at the rebuff.

"Like smuggling snow flowers?" Faryn called after him, holding up a red blossom he had plucked off a passing shipmate. The man frowned deeply, glancing around them. "You really should try to be a little more discreet."

"What exactly did my brother tell you?" He raised an

eyebrow at the trio.

"Just everything we needed to know to get to Hrinth." Adridia rested a hand on the hilt of her sword as she smirked.

"Why do you need to get to Hrinth so badly?" He squinted his eyes at them, suspicious of why five well-armed elves needed to leave Serradon right after the throne was taken.

"That's for us to know. As for the snow flowers, as long as we get to Hrinth, safely, I see no reason for the dock police to know about them." Peld nodded in understanding and defeat, knowing a raid by the dock police would be the end of his business, legitimate and illegitimate.

"The Lady Fair departs at noon tomorrow. I'll meet you here to escort you to the upper dock." He tipped his hat towards them then ventured towards his section of the dock where his crew was still loading cargo.

"I suppose we should try to find my brother and the witch," Faryn sighed and leaned his head back, drinking in the slight heat from the afternoon sun, a reprieve from the harsh winds of the mountain passes.

"I just need a fucking drink." Jerylia squared her shoulders and made her way back towards the town.

"Do you think she knows where she's going?" Adridia whispered to Faryn.

"Absolutely not," he replied before they both followed after the princess.

Chapter 8

Jerylia

"It's a good thing we're leaving today. There's a storm brewing over the mountains." Jerylia pulled her cloak tighter around her and eyed the dark clouds gathering in the distance. The streets of Shemon were crowded with people preparing for the long storm. The twins ducked inside of a bakery close to them while the three women went to see the butcher.

"We need as much dried meat as we can get for this." Gwera laid five gold coins on the wooden counter. The butcher's eyes widened and he silently ducked into the back of the store. He came out a moment later with a large paper parcel tied with twine. They smiled and thanked him before heading back out onto the busy street.

"I hope I don't get seasick," Jerylia groaned as they searched for the archers.

"Have you never been on a ship before?" Adridia looked shocked. The princess frowned at her.

"I'm the princess heir of Serradon. I may be the most prolific warrior princess of this generation but my mother would sooner chain me to my bed than let me go to sea," Gwera giggled.

"Very true." The warrior spotted the twins and waved them over.

"We should head towards the docks. We've got everything we need." Faryn shouldered a large canvas bag filled with provisions. Down the street, something clattered against the cobblestones. The princess whipped her head around to see a group of soldiers in black with red snakes stitched into the collars. They were grabbing people roughly by their cloaks, asking questions.

"Those are Sinisstra's soldiers." The blood drained from Gwera's face. "We need to get to the docks now." They all pulled their hoods further over their faces. Gwera whispered something to herself and her eyes glowed a gentle green.

"Don't make any sudden movements, that will only get their attention," Adridia said under her breath. Jerylia looked at the witch, whose brow was furrowed with concentration as her fingers twisted under her cloak.

"Gwera, are you cloaking us?" she asked, resting a hand on her friend's shoulder. "No, I'm just changing our faces. It's less suspicious." Her eyes flashed brighter for a moment before a glamour settled over her, changing her hair color to a soft brown and softening her features. They spaced themselves out so they weren't huddled together and began slowly strolling towards a side street that led to the docks. Jerylia gasped when someone grabbed the back of her hood, gripping her hair with it in their fist. She was spun around and came face to face with a Draerigean guard. He snarled in her face, his breath fanning over her.

"Have you seen this woman?" He held up a wrinkled piece of paper with her face on it. She was wanted, dead or alive. Gwera was right; Sinisstra had no need of her.

"T-that's the princess." She made her voice shake as if she was afraid. The guard smirked at her.

"A performer in Fraton identified her and told us she was coming here. Have you seen her?" He shoved the paper into her face.

"N-no, we haven't. Did the performer say anything else that might help identify her?" Her head was beginning to throb from the man's grip on her hair. The man smiled wickedly and released her.

"He won't be saying anything else, to anyone." Jerylia nodded and stepped away from him. "If you see the princess, alert your local Draerigean authorities, please." The soldier's boots were heavy on the cobblestones as he walked away.

"They tortured him and it was my fault." The princess leaned against the side of a building as realization crashed over her. Someone rested a hand on her shoulder and forced her chin up. She found herself gazing into Gwera's almost white eyes.

"It's not your fault. They had a picture of you. Anyone in Fraton could have told them that we spoke with the performer. You can't blame yourself for this." Gwera shut her eyes tight and pushed the heel of her hand against her head. "I can't hold the glamour for much longer so we need to go." The princess nodded but didn't move.

"She killed him. This was a mistake. I can't leave my mother here." She shook her head, tears welling in her eyes.

"We really need to get moving." Theal was bouncing on his toes, anxious to get moving.

"Jer, we gotta go. I'm gonna carry you." Adridia moved towards the princess.

"No!" she snapped. She took a deep breath and wiped her face with her arm before standing up straight. "I can do it. I have to be strong, for my mother." Her companions eyed her, warily.

"Peld should be waiting for us where we met him yesterday." Faryn's eyes were searching around them, looking for a route to the docks.

"Then let's go." Jerylia clenched her jaw and gripped the hilt of her sword before they began moving, swiftly, down the side street.

The coastal city of Fraton was in absolute chaos. Soldiers in black garb were everywhere, tossing people out of buildings and taking anything that caught their eye. The princess saw one man out of the corner of her eye refuse to answer the soldier in front of him. He still had a rebellious glint in his eye when the soldier cut his throat and let him bleed out on the cobblestone. She turned her head away before she could witness what they would do to the man's wife. She blocked out the ringing in her ears as anger filled her chest. Draerigean soldiers were destroying the lives of her people who she had sworn to protect and she was fleeing to Hrinth. She was leaving them here to suffer, helpless as their queen was lying in the dungeons of her own castle. She steeled her nerves, breathing through the panic. She was going to get help, she told herself, but nothing could erase the guilt that had settled in the pit of her stomach.

"I was beginning to think you wouldn't show." Peld cracked a smile when he saw them thundering down the docks.

"The soldiers from Draerige are here. We need to leave now." The princess tried to push past him.

"Wait a minute, why would they be here?" The companions glanced at each other. "They're looking for the princess." Peld furrowed his eyebrows in confusion, an expression that melted when his eyes landed on Jerylia. She was fast as lightning, with a dagger across his throat before he could even breathe.

"You say anything to anyone and you will forfeit your right to live, do you understand me?" The captain nodded. "I am going to Hrinth to find the only person capable of defeating Sinisstra and her dragons. I am not abandoning my country." She was desperate to prove to him that she was worthy of her crown, that she always would be. He needed to know she was leaving for help and would never abandon her country if she had any other choice. He nodded in understanding then pointed at the lift used to bring cargo to the upper docks.

"Then we'd better hurry and shove off." Jerylia stepped away but kept the dagger in her hand as a small warning. They followed the captain to the lift where he wrapped his hands around the lever.

"All of you get on and hang on to the ropes. This isn't going to be the most pleasant ride," he grunted and heaved the lever forward, sending the slab of wood under their feet lurching upward. The princess spread her feet to steady herself and gripped the rope like a vice with one hand. She slid her dagger back in her boot carefully and instinctively reached for Adridia next to her. The warrior didn't complain as Jerylia squeezed her arm tight enough to leave bruises. She closed her eyes as the lower dock got further away and the ropes groaned as they neared the upper dock. She had never been fond of high places. Her training as an assassin was the worst few years of her life as she was taught to climb the highest walls of the castle.

"Jer, we made it, you can let go of me now." Jerylia opened her eyes as Adridia attempted to peel her fingers off of her forearm. The princess nodded and removed her grip on both the warrior's arm and the rope holding up the lift. She sucked in a shaky breath as she quickly stepped onto the more stable upper dock. She leaned over the side to watch the ocean lap against the wooden stilts far below. She jumped when the captain jumped onto the docks next to them from the lift. He led them across the thin wooden plank that connected the dock to the top deck of the ship.

"Gather round, lads!" He called to his crew after using his fingers to let out a sharp whistle. His shipmates gathered around them, eyeing the petite witch and curvy princess with hunger. "This group of fine warriors is seeking safe passage to Hrinth.

They also know all about our, um, sensitive cargo." He grinned at his crew, most of whom were still eyeing the three women. "I would warn you to stay away from the women but I have a feeling they would rather you find out the hard way what happens when you mess with them." The boat rocked a little more as Adridia grinned and flexed her fingers, controlling the water beneath them. Gwera's eyes flashed green and little wisps of magic curled around her fingers. Jerylia just fingered the hilt of her sword, a small smile dancing on her lips. Most of the crew glanced away from them at that.

"We would like to make it to Hrinth unharmed or one of us may just let slip to the Hrinthian authorities exactly what kind of cargo you are transporting here." The princess grinned and pulled her dagger from her boot, spinning the blade expertly with her fingers. The crew around her just nodded. She saw a few with frowns on their faces, wringing their hands together, most likely plotting her death. "And we have no issue killing anyone who would harm us in any way." She glared at the crew.

"Let's get these fine folk to Hrinth then." The captain threw his hands up and his crew dispersed. It wasn't long before the ship was slowly moving out of the harbor, helped along with Adridia's control over the water beneath them.

"When we finally free Serradon," Jerylia began to say, "I am going to kill my mother," she finished before running to the edge of the boat to vomit over the side. "For never letting me on a boat!" She groaned and clutched her stomach with her hands.

"I'm not sharing a cabin with her," Faryn said, wrinkling his nose at her retching.

"Fuck you!" she called over her shoulder between bouts of sickness.

Chapter 9

Jerylia

"I hate boats. I hate the ocean. I hate it all." The princess wiped her mouth with the back of her hand and smacked her lips together to try and rid her mouth of the taste of vomit before turning back towards the upper deck. Many of the ship's crew had mocked her during that first week at sea and still did due to her lack of control over her stomach. "Does it ever get better?" she groaned as she rolled her shoulders back. Her stomach rolled as the ship rocked again.

"You'll get used to it eventually, though we're probably more likely to reach Hrinth before that happens," Faryn mocked her from where he sat, shirtless, on a nearby barrel, his skin already tanned after just a week at sea. The climate was growing warmer as they travelled south and the sun had been relentless. Jerylia's own skin had begun to turn red from the constant exposure.

"Oh fuck off." He just grinned as she faced Adridia and drew her sword again. The warrior gripped her own sword and gave her opponent a small smile.

"We'll be on land again before you know it, Jer." The princess spun her sword once, bending her knees so she could bounce on the balls of her feet.

"Thank Serra for that," she breathed before Faryn called the start of the match and the two women sprang into action.

Jerylia's sword shone in the sunlight as she swung it towards her most trusted friend. Adridia's own sword met it halfway, the sound of steel meeting steel ringing over the deck of the ship. Some of the shipmates gathered around to watch the two warriors duel. Jerylia was smaller than Adridia, a factor she used to her advantage, her feet quick and sure as she ducked under her opponent's sword. Adridia used her size and strength to send strong vibrations up Jerylia's arms when their blades met, momentarily shocking the smaller woman. Sweat gathered on the princess's forehead as the sun blazed down on them.

"How long has it been since you've won a spar against me? Face it, I've surpassed you." Adridia never faltered as she spoke.

"I was raised by one of the best warrior queens Serradon has ever seen and trained by her. She was a merciful queen but she was ruthless with my training," Jerylia countered, going into a complete offense mode, performing strike after strike, a blur of movement across the deck. Adridia blocked her the best she could but ended up sprawled on her back, her sword clattering across the wooden deck.

"Oh, this isn't over, Princess Bitch." Adridia stood, peeling off her soaked shirt. Jerylia did the same, leaving the two women with only a soft white band covering their breasts. Jerylia eyed the columns of muscles rippling across Adridia's abdomen and the thick cords of muscle lining her arms. Those were her two strongest points, the stability in her core and the strength of her arms allowed her to wield a much larger sword but it also meant she moved slower, giving Jerylia plenty of chances to duck around her and gain access to her weakest points such as the backs of her knees or her underarms. The men around them whistled and leered but the warrior and the princess couldn't care less.

"Oh, you want to lose again?" Jerylia taunted, bouncing on the balls of her feet again. Adridia flicked her eyes to Faryn who nodded and called the match. The women sprang at each other again, their exhaustion doing nothing to impact their ferocity.

"You've got the wrong idea if you think I'm going to lose again," Adridia taunted. Jerylia smirked. If Adridia thought she was going to distract the princess with meaningless banter, she had another thing coming. She stepped forward onto one foot, throwing her weight forward so she could spring behind the warrior. It was a move she had used a hundred times. Even if Adridia caught onto what she was doing, Jerylia was fast enough that it wouldn't matter. But Adridia moved fast, faster than Jerylia had anticipated, and caught the end of her braid. The princess let out a short yelp at the sharp pain in her scalp. Adridia brought her sword up and Jerylia lurched forward, the pressure at the back of her head suddenly gone. She whirled around to see her most trusted friend holding several inches of her chestnut locks.

"You cut my hair!" Adridia's smile melted as Jerylia swung at her with her sword. She barely had time to parry and her distraction gave Jerylia the chance to pull out her dagger and point it at her friend's throat in a split second. Adridia didn't move but she also knew that Jerylia would never harm her like that. "I told you I didn't want to cut my hair," her voice cracked.

"You're too recognizable with it. We had to." Faryn had moved from his perch and was now standing behind the princess.

"So both of you conspired to cut my hair without my knowledge," the princess seethed, her fingers shaking around the hilt of the dagger at Adridia's throat. Tears welled in her eyes as another wave of nausea built in her stomach. "I don't have my magic yet. That was the only connection I still had with my mother. 'Queens wear their hair long' is what she always used to tell me when I complained about the tangles. It was one of the things we shared and now I don't know what's happened to her." The dagger clattered against the wooden planks as Jerylia fell to the deck, fighting the vomit rising in her throat and her lungs constricted. She gasped for air as panic rose in her chest, stealing her breath.

"I'm sorry, Jerylia. It had to be done. It'll grow back." Adridia crouched and laid a comforting hand on her back. The princess squeezed her eyes shut against the wave of sickness. She forced her mind to calm and pulled in a deep breath, her hands shaking as she rose to her feet.

"I know. I know I'm being ridiculous. I'm just disappointed my magic hasn't made an appearance yet." Jerylia hadn't felt even a whisper of her magic since her twenty-sixth birthday. She hadn't felt the calling of trees when she had been in the mountains, the forest hadn't sung to her. Her mother had always described it as a song, every single time. She had told Jerylia that the earth sang a different song than the life that grew from it and different plants had different songs. She'd said the power of the queens was like learning how to sing along, changing a few notes at a time.

"It will. We're going to find the dragonslayer and we're going to free Serradon from Sinisstra. You will be reunited with your mother again." Jerylia nodded as the nausea subsided. Heavy footsteps across the deck had them all turning to see Peld approaching.

"I'm afraid I have bad news for you." The captain wrang his hands together nervously. "There's a storm system up ahead. I've been tasting it on the air for a few days now and hoped it would dissipate or move but it hasn't." Storm sensing is a useful power for a sailor.

"What does that mean?" Faryn asked.

"We'll be arriving in Hrinth a few days later than planned." He glanced at the seasick princess who was looking greener by the second, an arm pressed against her stomach. "Storm should hit in a few hours so, unless you enjoy being soaked to the bone, I suggest you all take shelter below deck and let us take care of getting through it." They all nodded and joined Gwera and Theal in Jerylia's cabin. The princess immediately curled up on the bed with her face near the edge, a bucket just below her.

"Great, we're stuck on this stupid boat for *longer*." She groaned, lurching over the side of the bed to heave into the bucket. Gwera wrinkled her nose.

"Storm on the horizon?" She asked. Faryn nodded.

"Captain said it would delay us only a few days." Jerylia scoffed at that.

"Only! Every day we're stuck on this goddess-damned boat, my mother is stuck in her own castle answering to a *monster*." She coughed as she wiped the back of her mouth with her hand.

"It's not like we can go around, that would take longer. And it's too much for Adridia to try to control, even her immense power is nothing compared to a natural storm," Gwera explained. Jerylia flopped onto her back, the bed frame groaning beneath her. She closed her eyes and covered them with her hands, fighting back tears

"It's okay to be upset, Jer." She turned her head to look at Faryn. "Not just about your mother and father. But also about your prince." His eyes were soft as he gazed at her, love still shone in them.

"Why would I be upset about him? It's not like I loved him," her voice cracked and she cringed, recalling their last night together. She hadn't lied when she'd told him she loved him but she didn't want anyone else to know. It was their moment and it felt wrong to share it with anyone else.

"You only knew each other for a short time, but any fool could see that you cared for him and him for you. It doesn't make you weak to admit that you're heartbroken over him. It actually makes you stronger than the monster that killed him." She was silent as Adridia laid down beside her and wrapped her arms around her. The princess just stared at the ceiling, a storm of emotions passing through her. Grief, for the lives of her father and her prince. Anxiety, over leaving her mother behind in the clutches of Sinisstra. Most importantly, rage. Rage was burning a hole in her chest. She was angry that Sinisstra thought the former empress was weak. She was angry that Sinisstra had turned her sights toward Serradon, towards Jerylia's home. She was angry that Sinisstra had killed her father, the only man she had ever truly loved with her whole heart. She let the anger sit there, festering in her chest.

"I hate her," she hissed. "I hate that bitch of an empress." Her voice filled with poison. "I'm not going to stop fighting until my sword pierces her heart." She sat up and took out her dagger, drawing it across her palm until blood dripped onto the wooden floor. "I swear on my father's life."

The cabin was silent as Jerylia tore a strip of cloth from the hem of her shirt and wrapped it around her hand, wincing at the slight sting. Her hand pulsed as blood flowed to the fresh wound.

"I'm beginning to think we have another problem," Theal said from the corner where he was examining the tips of his arrows. "Even if we do find the dragonslayer, he has no stake in this war. How are we going to convince him to risk his life fighting for a country that made him feel like he didn't belong?"

"Shit. I didn't even think of that." Jerylia buried her head in her hands. "I guess we just have to hope that he still feels loyalty towards Serradon. Or threaten him if he doesn't."

"This is the elf that killed all of Hrinth's dragons. I don't think threatening him is going to work." Gwera was weaving magic between her fingers, the green wisps casting a glow on her face.

"Then we offer him a reward. Goods, jewels, land." Jerylia clenched her fist around the strip of cloth. "Hell, I'll even make him consort to the queen if that's what it takes. Anything to get Sinisstra out of my castle."

"You'd really do that?" The princess flinched at the hurt in Faryn's voice.

"The only elf I ever came close to loving is dead." She steadied herself and took a deep breath. "Yeah, I would make him consort to the queen to save my people. I would sacrifice my right to a marriage out of love to save Serradon." Her companions were silent for a moment.

"Jer, will you sing the Ballad of the Goddesses?" Theal asked from his corner. "No one sings it as you do." The princess nodded and found the song in her head, feeling it in her blood.

The triplet goddesses, o'er us they reign. We were gifted the land by Asayda's hand.

With a sweep of her fingertips, she formed mountains and valleys.

The world slowed around her as her voice flowed from her soul, haunted and broken.

Eowessa watches over the people with an ever protective eye. She lends an ear to our pleas and deals justice with a fair hand. Serra guards the throne and protects our merciful

queens. She delivers life and death and rules the goddesses three. This is our history, these are our guardians, these are our mothers.

A chill settled over the princess as she sang about her ancestor.

"I don't know who wrote that song but only one of the lines rhymes. It's like they gave up on the rhyming and just decided to tell the story of the goddesses." Adridia had always despised the famous ballad. She didn't care for music like her companions did, never quite understood how the melody tells more of the story than the words do. Jerylia had always felt a special connection to music, possibly a result of her lineage. If the earth truly did sing, Serra's gift would help her listen and give her the necessary skills to sing along.

"It's a ballad, it doesn't have to rhyme," the warrior snorted.

"It's the shortest ballad I've ever heard." She stretched out on the bed behind Jerylia. "I can sing the long version if you want me to but it's two hours long," the princess teased, pinching Adridia below her ribs. Adridia retaliated immediately, pinching the sensitive skin of her neck. The princess squealed and tucked her head against her shoulders.

"I'd rather you run me through with your sword," she whined dramatically. Jerylia laughed before a wave of nausea hit her and she heaved into the bucket again, stomach rolling at the smell that wafted back up.

"Just a couple more days, Little Serra." Gwera threaded her magic through Jerylia's thick hair, gathering it into a bun at the nape of her neck while Adridia tied it. The princess just groaned into the bucket.

Chapter 10

Theal

The desert skyline was a sight to behold as *The Lady Fair* pulled into the main port in Kher on the island of Hrinth. Domed buildings dotted the streets, vendors set up between them. People stared at the foreigners as they got off the ship, the sun beaming down on them. Sweat immediately coated Theal's body, soaking into his thick shirt.

"We need new clothes." Jerylia was the first to speak as she eyed the locals dressed in light-colored shifts and tunics. Theal spied a vendor a few blocks down with bundles of light-colored material laid out in front of him.

"There," he pointed. Hrinthians moved out of their way as they travelled down the street, eyeing them suspiciously. They stood out from not only their strange clothing but also their skin. Hrinth was mostly a desert which was not the ideal environment for mountain elves. Their skin burned too easily in the sun. Dark elves were created for desert life, from their dark grey skin to their silk-like hair that easily withstood sun damage. He could spot a few lighter-skinned elves that seemed to be merchants near the docks.

"We need clothes," Gwera smiled sweetly at the vendor. The witch was usually their bargainer, less prone to anger than the rest of them and less intimidating from her small size and kind face. Her eyes were the only thing that caught people off guard, a beautiful shade of ice blue, almost white. The vendor glanced at the rest of the warriors, all foreboding with violent eyes.

"I'm sorry, I don't sell to foreigners." He moved to close his shutters, flinching when Jerylia slammed a handful of gold coins on the counter.

"How about now?" He eyed the coins before scooping them up and dumping them into his satchel.

"I believe you'll find these to your liking." He motioned to the front edge of the table. Gwera picked up a white shift that cinched at the waist and would end at her knees. Jerylia picked up a matching one in a pale blue and Adridia grabbed a light green one. Theal and Faryn both grabbed thin tunics that had been dyed a light tan color. "And you'll want the matching headscarves to prevent sunstroke or sunskin." He held out swaths of fabric that matched the clothes in their hands along with five pairs of leather sandals.

"Thank you." Gwera smiled at him again before leading them to a dark alcove where they could easily change. The twins turned their backs to the three women as they pulled off their heavy winter clothes and pulled on the lighter desert clothing. Theal sucked in a breath when he turned around and saw Adridia in the tight shift. It had come down to Gwera's knees but only came down to the taller elf's mid-thigh. Her arms were exposed, revealing the wave tattoo that covered her entire right arm. He glanced away before she noticed the way he looked at her. Jerylia's shift came to just above her knee, allowing her tattoo depicting the goddess Serra on her left thigh to peek out when she moved. He also caught a glimpse of the smoking sword on her forearm when she lifted her hands to secure her headscarf. The witch was the most imposing of all of them with the dark whorls of the old language that wrapped around both of her arms and legs. She would never tell them what they said, only that they were extremely powerful and boosted her magic. Theal looked down at his own arm, covered in a flock of birds.

"What are we going to do with our old clothes?" Adridia asked as she secured her scabbard around her waist.

"Gwera knows a spell," Jerylia commented as she strapped her dagger to her thigh, yanking on the strap to make sure it was secure. Gwera whispered over her discarded cloak, fingers twisting in front of her. Her eyes glowed and green sparks floated down from her fingertips. The cloak shifted and changed until there was a black satchel sitting where her cloak had been. The witch then gathered up all of their clothes and shoved them into the satchel.

"What is that?" Theal asked as he slung his bow and quiver over his shoulders.

"A bottomless satchel." She grinned as she slung it over her shoulder.

"Neat trick," Faryn smirked as he tied his shoulder-length hair back into a loose knot to keep it off his neck before looping the scarf around his head.

"It's a simple spell but it's very draining." The witch wiped her forehead with the back of her hand. Sweat shone on her neck from both the heat and magic exertion. She breathed in deep through her nose and stuck her tongue out to taste the air. "The magic is different here." She recoiled visibly at the feeling of it. "These lands aren't governed by the triplet goddesses. They're ruled by a lone goddess, Della."

"Will the magic affect my powers, Gwera?" Adridia asked, curling her hand against her chest. The warrior had always had the most impressive powers of the three. She came from a long line of water summoners; the Ibyrs were well known in Serradon.

It was awe-striking to watch the warrior bend the liquid into whatever she wanted.

"I don't know. The air, it's sharper, more reactive. The magic in Serradon is much older so it's subtler, and won't be as prone to react to emotional distress. Your powers might be more susceptible to emotions so be careful." She pinned the princess with a sharp gaze. "Especially you. I can see it in your eyes. You feel the calling. You need to tread carefully." Jerylia snapped her attention back to the witch and nodded excitedly. Her cerulean eyes sparkled with excitement. Theal's heart warmed. He had not seen that look in her eyes for too long.

"The earth sings," she whispered.

"We need to find information about the dragonslayer." Theal glanced at the mouth of the alley, people bustling by.

"Time to search our favorite places." Adridia grinned with a devilish glint in her eye.

"Of course you would use it as an excuse to drink," Gwera chuckled as they entered the busy street.

"Perhaps we should split up?" Theal offered, glancing at the blonde warrior and nearly melted at the expression on her face. She held his heart, his soul, every part of him and she didn't even know it. His heart twisted in his chest and he forced himself to look away.

"Adri can go with the twins while Gwere and I go together," Jerylia offered. Adridia opened her mouth to argue against it.

"Before you spout some bull-headed nonsense about needing to protect Jerylia, know I can protect her and she can protect herself." Gwera interrupted the warrior.

Adridia frowned and began to argue anyway. "No." She glanced at the archers and the warrior. "And if we leave you to your own devices, you three have ways of gleaning information that Jerylia and I can't use." She smirked at them. Faryn grinned and cracked his neck.

"Say no more. Me and my magic cock are on it." He clapped his twin on the shoulder. Theal rolled his eyes but a small smile still danced on his lips. His twin truly never learned when to keep his mouth shut.

"I didn't say it was magic," Gwera said, deadpanned.

"I think the women of Serradon would disagree with you." He winked at her as she grimaced.

"You're disgusting." She looped her arm with Jerylia's.

"You'll miss me while we're apart though." He blew her a kiss and she rolled her eyes.

"Don't kid yourself, Faryn," the princess replied.

"Meet at that tavern over there, let's say, three days?" Theal asked the others, jerking his head towards the tavern across the street.

"We'll be there," Gwera shouted over her shoulder as the pair disappeared into the crowd. Faryn rested his fists on his hips and breathed deeply through his nose as he scanned the busy street, his gaze snagging on a few young women.

"I have a magic cock." Theal rolled his eyes at his twin.

"You do not have a magic cock," he dismissed Faryn as they pushed through the crowd.

"Why don't we make a bet then? Whoever gets the location of the dragonslayer first is owed ten gold pieces." Faryn cocked an eyebrow at his brother.

"You're on, cock-wielder," Adridia sneered at Faryn before Theal could reply. She glanced at both of them, a hand clasped on each of their shoulders. "You forget about your most important competition, Fare." She shoved them both aside before sauntering into the closest tavern, pulling the front of her shift down to reveal the swell of her breasts.

"Theal, do you ever fear that you just might not be worthy of her?" His brother slung an arm around his shoulders as they followed the warrior. Theal knew the question wasn't spiteful or meant to wound him in any way. His brother was just jesting as he always did.

"Oh, I am definitely not worthy of her," Theal chuckled as they entered the dim light of the tavern.

"They said they would be here. Just be patient," Theal chided his impatient twin. Faryn grumbled and tapped his fingers on the table in front of him before calling over the serving girl to order a plate of dinner.

"I'm being patient." He glanced at Adridia who was still counting out the twenty gold pieces she had won from their bet. "Do you have to do that now?" he snapped at her. She rolled her eyes at him and scooped the coins into her purse.

"Someone is a little bit grumpy," she whispered to Theal, a humorous gleam in her eye. His heart skipped a beat at her smile.

"He's been away from his lady love for too long." Theal joked, hiding his reaction to her nearness. He flinched when his twin lodged a dagger in the table, inches from his fingers. "Watch it," Theal ground out, anger flaring in his chest. Faryn pointed an accusing finger at him.

"You watch it. We let them go off alone. They could be dead for all we know and it would be our fault." He plucked the dagger out of the splintered wood and twirled it in his fingers.

"We're not dead." Faryn's eyes nearly popped out of his skull as Jerylia slid into the chair next to him.

"But you might end up that way if you imply one more time that we aren't capable of protecting ourselves," Gwera said sweetly as she took a seat next to Adridia.

"So what information did you glean with your magic cock?" Jerylia asked, tilting her head slightly to the side. Faryn just glared at Adridia who leaned forward and grinned.

"Go on, say it." She nudged his shoulder. He sighed heavily, reluctance dripping from that one breath.

"My cock is not magic."

"Then who had the magic genitals?" Jerylia asked.

"I have a magic twat," Adridia stated proudly. Theal smiled. Of course, she did.

Everything about her was magical.

"So what did you find out, because no one would tell us anything. They just laughed at us and told us to get lost in the desert."

"We have to talk to someone named Sevag in a town called Djat. He can tell us where to go." Jerylia sighed, cradling her head in her hands.

"Of course it's not easy. Why would it be easy? I just want this mess to be over with," she groaned.

"Just drink and forget about it." Faryn handed her a crudely made goblet filled to the brim with cheap wine. She cracked a smile and drank deeply from it.

Chapter 11

Jerylia

"Wake up, drunk," Jerylia groaned as someone prodded her side. She pulled the blanket over her face and curled onto her side, fighting the dryness in her throat and ignoring the pounding in her head. "Get up." The finger poked her ribs again. Jerylia's eyes snapped open and she recoiled at the bright light.

"Why did you let me drink so much?" she whined as she sat up.

"We had to cut you off." Gwera sat next to her and began brushing Jerylia's hair. "I know you're dealing with a lot right now, princess, but we need to keep a straight head." Her tone was soft as she twisted the chestnut locks into a thick plait. "I think you should abstain from drinking for a while. I've seen drunks and I don't want you to become one." The princess sighed and glanced at her friend. She knew why the witch feared for her. The pain in her heart lessened with alcohol and she could easily see herself slipping off the edge of sobriety to cover the pain. But drinking wouldn't bring Kaed or her father back and it wouldn't help them take her kingdom back. She could wait until she was home in her castle to drink to her heart's content.

"If that would make you feel better I will limit myself." The witch gave her a soft smile.

"Thank you." She glanced at the door. "We need to get moving. Djat is a couple of hours' journey from here and we need to find transportation." She stood and handed Jerylia her scabbard, the hilt of her sword glittering in the sunlight, which she quickly secured around her waist before following Gwera out into the busy streets.

"Ah, she lives." Faryn cracked a smile at her as she blinked in the light of the rising sun. She gave him a vulgar gesture to which he just laughed.

"What do the elves in the south use for transportation across the desert?" Adridia asked. Gwera spotted something a few blocks down and smiled brightly.

"Ishtuks," she breathed, quickening her pace. Jerylia spotted the animals as soon as they neared. Ishtuks looked like giant birds with long legs and necks connected by a giant bulbous body covered in sand-colored feathers. They had small heads that looked to be mostly beak and eyes that were constantly swiveling around.

"What is that?" Theal wrinkled his nose at the giant creatures.

"It's an Ishtuk. They're giant birds!" Gwera exclaimed, reaching up to pet the closest one. It made a low chirping noise as it pressed its head into her hand. "They can't fly but they can run like hell." She looked around, trying to spot the owner of the huge birds.

"Hey, guys?" They all glanced at Adridia. "Should we worry about that?" She pointed down the crowded street. Jerylia's heart thundered in her chest as she spotted a group of finely dressed men with a red sun emblazoned on their jackets.

"Those are Hrinthian royal guards." The guard in the head of the group spotted the princess and began shouting, the guards sprinting towards them.

"Princess Jerylia Serra of Serradon," the guards placed two

fingers against their brows, a Hrinthian gesture between warriors. "The king requests your presence at the royal palace in Isef." Isef was the sister city of Kher, just a few miles away along the coast.

It was the shining jewel of Hrinth and home to the royal family. Jerylia eyed the guards warily, her hand wrapping around the hilt of her sword.

"And if we refuse?" she asked cautiously. The guard's eyes flicked downward, noting the hand on her blade.

"I'm afraid you don't have a choice, your highness," he nearly spat her title. The polite smile disappeared from his face and the man who had greeted her as a warrior was gone, replaced by this elf who would kill her without question if she threatened him. She nodded and agreed to go with them if only to spare them from a deadly skirmish in the busy streets where an innocent bystander might be put in harm's way. They were led to a large, ornate carriage pulled by camels. The guards themselves didn't join the squadron inside the carriage but took up posts on the outside.

"How long are we going to be stuck inside this thing?" Faryn was glancing at the small windows in the doors and the rear of the carriage. He banged on the glass with his fist, startling the guards sitting at the rear-facing bench behind them. "How long to Isef?" The guards ignored him, turning back towards the road behind them.

"All the more heavily populated cities lie along the coast. The ocean breeze cools them and makes them a bit more habitable and the Hrinthians use the water to power some of the important grain mills," Jerylia informed them while she inspected her dagger. She looked up when she felt all her eyes on her. "What?"

"I didn't know you actually paid attention in your studies, or that you attended at all," Gwera teased. Jerylia rolled her eyes.

"I fully accepted the duties of being queen and that includes being knowledgeable of the countries closest to Serradon." She now spun her dagger in her hand, the movement taking little effort as the blade moved like silk over her palm. "I speak six languages, you know."

"Did you ever think about what would become of us when you were crowned queen?" Theal asked the question from a place of genuine curiosity, not malice.

"I would have kept Adridia on as my personal guard and Right Hand of the Queen. Gwera would have been put in charge of the witch's faction. It's high time the people learned to respect witches instead of fearing them." The redhead grinned as green wisps of power slithered through her hair. "Theal would have become my Captain of the Royal Guard and Faryn would have overseen the archer's faction," the princess listed as she stared out the window at the passing desert.

"You sound as if you've made these decisions long ago," Faryn commented. Her blue eyes were sharpened steel as she met his gaze, never once faltering.

"I've known since the day I met each one of you." Theal and Faryn she had known since childhood and her mother had expressed the bright future she had seen for them. Adridia and Jerylia had met when the princess was just a teenager and the warrior was barely eighteen, hating each other at first, but the princess had seen the fierceness in the warrior's eyes and had not balked. Gwera, she had met by chance and had instantly been drawn to the older elf, almost twenty years older than the princess, they had been fast friends.

"When did you become so wise, Little Serra?" Adridia nudged the princess with her shoulder, attempting to lighten the mood. Jerylia forced a smile, her thoughts drifting to her mother back home.

"Gwera must be rubbing off on me." The princess shrugged and turned back to the small window as a city appeared far away on the horizon.

"What did you learn about the king during your studies?" Theal asked.

"He's very old, seven hundred and fifty-four, I think. He's been on the throne for hundreds of years. He has three children, a son and two daughters. The eldest daughter was mated off in a political arrangement, the son is mated and next in line for the throne, and the youngest daughter is unmated," Jerylia listed. "He has no single mate, she died giving birth to his youngest daughter. Once the king's consort dies, he forms a harem. This particular king has a rather large one of almost four hundred men and women." Faryn drew a sharp breath.

"At seven hundred and fifty-four? There's no way he's getting full use of that." Faryn leaned back on the small carriage bench.

"We're almost there." Jerylia leaned forward gazing at the city, palm trees guarding the towering gates. She closed her eyes, a slight buzz under her skin. She opened herself up to it and the humming grew louder. It wasn't quite the song her mother had described but she felt comfort in the fact that the song had made itself known to her at last.

"What do you suppose the king wants?" Adridia asked.

"We're about to find out," Gwera said ominously as they passed through the gates at last, the iron wheels of the carriage rattling across cobblestones.

Though the sun beat down on the dusty streets, a cool breeze swept through the alleys from the ocean. The princess closed her eyes for a moment, breathing in the smell of salt and sand. She opened her eyes and gazed at the beautiful architecture of the city from the steps of the grand palace. The buildings were made of beautifully carved sandstone and white marble. Many of the larger buildings had thick columns that rose in the entrances, perhaps leftover from the more ancient Hrinthians. They didn't use the domed design the Kher used, instead most buildings and homes seemed to be stacked on top of one another, carved staircases winding this way and that. Jerylia could easily see why the city was called the shining jewel of Hrinth. They had every reason to be proud of this beautiful place.

"Greetings." Her eyes snapped towards the overly cheerful voice that greeted them. Its owner was a tall, thin man with shoulder-length russet hair and a sly smile stretched across his lips. He had slate grey skin dotted with dark freckles. His smile seemed genuine but there was a glint in his eyes that made her hesitate to trust him. He had his hands clasped behind his back and his shoulders were draped with an elegant red jacket, silver thread woven throughout. Two women stood behind him, both with the same grey skin and dark, silky hair that most Hrinthians boasted. He beckoned them forward. "I am the crown prince Griel and this is my mate, Raenya." He motioned to the smaller woman whose hand rested on her swollen stomach protectively. She only nodded at the visitors, her mouth set in a straight line. "This is my sister, Princess Maori." The princess was taller than her brother's mate and seemed more muscular than both her brother and his mate. What was most shocking were her eyes, like molten fire. She smiled and Jerylia found herself drawn to the warmth in her expression. She could already tell Maori and her were going to get along fabulously.

"Welcome to Hrinth, formally," she greeted the squadron,

her eyes ablaze with curiosity.

"We'll show you to your rooms. Our father is expecting you and you can't meet him dressed like that." Jerylia glanced down at the dirt-stained shift she was wearing. It was several days dirty, as was she and she knew they all smelled like it. Embarrassment suddenly flooded through her.

They swiftly turned around and led the group into the vast palace. The windows of the palace held no glass and there were only doorways, no doors to be shut as they strolled through the lower levels of the palace. Silk curtains hung near the windows and doorways, swaying in the gentle breeze. The palace was carved from the same sandstone and marble as the rest of the city but beautiful colored tiles covered the floor in tiny squares. She examined it further to see that the colors weren't just random, together they created a beautiful image of a coastal city backed by a golden desert. It wasn't until they got to the third floor that they saw a wooden door cracked open to let a breeze through the room. Jerylia counted each turn and stairway they came across until finally, the foreign royals halted.

"This is where you'll be staying. The bathing room is at the end of the hall. We'll come to gather you when our father is ready to meet you." Jerylia bowed diplomatically as they walked away, leaving the five of them to settle into their rooms.

Her room was magnificent. Arched windows-without-glass overlooked the ocean, the beat of the waves against the sandstone cliffs a steady rhythm. Long gauzy curtains hung from them, swaying in the breeze. There was a shallow pit that held a couch built into the low wall all the way around the large circle, pillows nestled into the cushions. The four-poster bed sat on a raised dais, with shimmering blue blankets edged with gold and thin curtains draped from the top of the wooden loop high above the mattress.

She ran her hand over the carved dresser, her fingernails catching on the grooves. The pit in her stomach was forgotten as she took in the beauty of this place. She had a moment of peace before the doors flew open and servants rushed in, pulling at her clothes.

"What are you doing?" she asked, they just replied in angry Hrinthian, their tongues rolling over the syllables. "What are you doing?" Her tone was hard as she repeated the question, in Hrinthian. They paused and glanced at each other, one of them explaining they needed to prepare her for the king. She nodded and unbelted her sword and dagger from around her waist, laying them gently on the bed. "Don't touch those." Her voice gave no room for argument.

"Come to the bathing room with us, princess," one of them requested. Jerylia nodded and padded down the hall after them. Steam wafted out the doors when they opened them. Shelves lined the walls, unopened bottles of soaps and oils covering every inch. A pool was carved into the floor, large enough to fit twenty people with plenty of space between them. Gwera already sat up to her neck in the steaming water, her red hair being lathered with shampoo.

"Get in," another of her servants ordered. The princess shrugged and tugged off her shift, slipping off her sandals with her toes. She paused, waiting for the servants to look away but they just tapped their feet with impatience. A blush bloomed on her cheeks as she untied the white band around her breasts and slid out of the tight undershorts, leaving her utterly bare to the world. No one but her mother, Gwera, and Adridia had seen her naked. Her servants were required to leave her before she bathed back in Serradon and no males were allowed to see her with the exception of her future consort. She nearly moaned as she slid into the water, the heat soothing her sore muscles. Two of the servants attending her slid into the water with her, their white shifts becoming almost transparent. They quickly went to work. The two in the water scrubbed her skin until it was red while another two untied her hair and plunged their hands into it. Adridia joined them not long after, a grimace on her face at the idea of being washed. Unlike Gwera, the warrior did not enjoy being pampered. She believed in short baths, just enough time to get clean. Time spent in a bath could be time spent training.

"It's not so bad, Adri," the princess offered her a smile, through clenched teeth.

"Liar," she hissed, but a smile danced on her lips nonetheless. She glanced around the room.

"Where are Faryn and Theal?" she asked.

"They requested to be bathed separately from you. They are in another wing." One of the servants replied. Jerylia relayed the information.

"I didn't know you could speak Hrinthian." Gwera raised a wine-colored eyebrow in shock.

"I'm smarter than I look," the princess smirked as the servants rinsed her hair before fanning it out across the tile behind her to allow it to dry faster. She watched as they wheeled in three fashion dummies, each draped in a different dress. Jerylia was silent as they pulled her from the water and began to lather her in lotion after drying her with a soft towel, while one began pulling the dress off the dummy. It was a gorgeous shade of cream with two panels of cloth that wrapped around her neck in a loop and covered her breasts before wrapping around into a full skirt that draped down to her feet with a white silk sash to cinch the waist. A cape was sewn into the neck, one that would cover her shoulders but leave the rest of her arms bare and end at the hem of the gown.

"I am not wearing that thing," Adridia argued with the servants who were holding a red dress towards her.

"Adri!" The warrior closed her mouth at Jerylia's sharp tone. "We are guests."

She sighed and allowed the servants to continue. The red fabric seemed to flow from two metal details on the shoulders, meeting between her breasts at a wide belt that matched the details of the shoulders. Two swaths of fabric flowed down her back from the shoulder pieces, swaying with her every movement. She smiled to herself at the disgruntled expression on the warrior's face. Adridia had always hated dresses. She claimed they left her too exposed and she could never fight properly in one. Back home, she usually opted for a split skirt and corset over a puffy shirt as her formal wear.

"I shall savor this moment forever." Gwera looked stunning in her light blue. A metal band wrapped around her throat and from that, a panel of gauzy fabric stretched over her chest, leaving her back bare. The fabric pooled around her feet and a thin metal belt wrapped around her waist.

"Leave your hair down. Unmated elves never tie their hair up." One of the servants slapped her hand as she reached up to braid her still wet hair. The now shoulder-length locks were already returning to their natural wavy state. They all whirled toward the door as Maori entered, sandals shuffling over the tiled floors, Faryn and Theal right behind her in dashing linen tunics cut perfectly to accentuate their broad shoulders and thin waists.

"My father is ready for you."

The throne room was just as grand as the rest of the palace, gold pillars lined the wide pathway that led to the throne. The throne itself seemed to be woven out of gold threads, knitted close together in the seat then getting sparser as they spread, the image strikingly similar to the sun. An ancient dark elf sat on the throne, his skin darker than both his children due to his age and carved with wrinkles. His braided hair reached his ankles and his eyes, oh Goddess, his eyes. They swirled with centuries of knowledge. He sat up straighter as they approached.

"Greetings, Princess Jerylia Serra of Serradon," he smiled, a few teeth missing. "You're a long way from home."

Chapter 12

Jerylia

"Your majesty." Jerylia kneeled, her head bowed, showing the king the respect he was owed. "The newly crowned Empress, Sinisstra Drae, has conquered the capital city of Serradon. Queen Aselidda is being held captive against her will. My squadron and I barely made it out alive," she explained.

"Rise, Princess." Jerylia stood to her full height once again. "We know of the terrors the Empress has brought upon Cordava. We are prepared to grant you asylum, should you agree to a few conditions. You must stay on the palace grounds, if you wish to leave you must be escorted by the guard. We are celebrating the Festival of Fish in three days' time and would be delighted for you to join us."

"That's very kind of you. We would be delighted." Jerylia smiled warmly at the elderly king.

"My children will escort you back to your rooms." Three young elves, two female and one male, emerged from behind the pillars, all wearing paper-thin gossamer shifts. They surrounded the king and escorted him out of the throne room. The prince and princess stepped forward and motioned for the five companions to go with them.

"Enjoy the rest of your evening," Griel said with no smile as he left them at the hall that housed their rooms.

"I would love to give you a tour of the palace and the

surrounding city tomorrow if you'd like to." Maori was all smiles as she stayed behind to converse with Jerylia. It was clear the young princess wasn't used to having royal guests, especially ones with such a vastly different culture. She was clearly curious to know more about them.

"That would be amazing, thank you." Her eyes glowed as she glanced down at Jerylia's muscled arms and the numerous scars that littered them. The princess' journey as a warrior would forever be marked on her body.

"I would also like to spar with you. You could teach me the fighting techniques of Serradon and I could teach you our fighting style." Jerylia smiled brightly as the princess stumbled over the words in Serradonian.

"I would love that," Jerylia replied in Hrinthian, the words rolling off her tongue, the language less sharp and guttural than the language of her homeland.

"Until the sun rises." Maori touched two fingers to her brow as she said her goodbye.

"Until the sun rises." Jerylia had always adored the Hrinthian goodbye. A blush crept up her neck as her stomach rumbled, the sound nearly echoing through the hall.

"I'll have dinner sent to your rooms," the princess offered.

"Just have it all sent to mine. We prefer to dine together." Maori nodded at Jerylia before she walked away, her footsteps clicking on the marble floor. The princess of Serradon breathed a sigh of relief before heading towards her room. Her companions were already relaxing in the cushioned pit with easy smiles on their faces.

"Princess Maori is having dinner brought up to us." Jerylia shifted her feet as she spoke, her white dress rippling from the movement. Adridia had changed already into the loose pants that cinched at the ankles and loose shirt that hemmed just below her ribs with long sleeves that cinched at the wrists that most Hrinthians favored for casual wear. The twins had unbuttoned their tunics, exposing the white shirts beneath and Gwera wore a thin linen dress dyed a rosy color.

"I've never seen you act so diplomatic, Jer. It was very becoming," Adridia joked, the rest of them laughing with her. Jerylia managed a chuckle as she strode to the carved dresser and pulled out an outfit similar to Adridia's in a soft shade of lavender.

"You were there when I greeted the foreign princes, Adri. I was diplomatic then," Jerylia countered as she opened the paper modesty screen so she could change her clothes. She struggled to reach the ties on the back of her dress.

"Yes, but I figured that was mostly your mother speaking. I had no idea you had a head for diplomacy." Her arms went limp and she threw her head back as a sigh of frustration heaved from her lips.

"We only ever see her diplomatic side when it involves stabbing," she heard them chuckle.

"Adri, could you please help me out of this cursed dress?" she finally asked her friend for help. The warrior heaved a sigh and the princess heard the rustle of clothing before Adridia appeared around the edge of the screen. Jerylia turned and gathered her hair over one shoulder as her friend began to loosen the ties under the cape. "Thank you." The warrior stalked back to the cushioned pit as Jerylia slid out of the dress and pulled on the casual attire. There was a soft knock on the door as she emerged from behind the modesty screen, her hair hanging freely in soft brown waves to her shoulder blades.

"Dinner, your highness." A female servant bowed her head

as Jerylia opened the door.

"Thank you. You may leave now," she replied in Hrinthian. The servant scuttled away, leaving a cart piled with platters of roasted poultry and grilled vegetables. She wheeled the cart inside, thrusting the door shut with a nudge of her hip.

"I want to talk about the king's orders to stay inside." Jerylia finally spoke once the wine had been poured and plates had been settled on laps. "I find it suspicious," she said around a mouthful of spiced poultry.

"Maybe he just wants to keep us safe," Faryn offered, his eyes never leaving the plate in his lap.

"Or he's plotting with Sinisstra," Gwera countered.

"She's winning. She has an army. She has her dragons. She has the power to raise the dead with a simple wave of her hand. Just as I am descended from a goddess, she is descended from a god," Jerylia said, her words barely more than a breath. "Right now, it appears she is winning. The king may be siding with her and selling me out because he thinks she will be merciful to him."

"She won't be. Cordava won't be enough for her. She'll want more," Theal realized, his eyes going wide.

"We have to stop her. Which means escaping this palace before Sinisstra finds out we're here." Jerylia finished her food and deposited the plate on the cushion next to her. She wrapped her fingers around the ornate goblet on the ledge behind her and crossed one knee over the other, leaning back.

"We could escape during the festival. It would be easy to slip a simple sleeping potion into the guards' drinks during the clamor of the feast," Gwera offered.

"We have three days to prepare. Tomorrow we'll explore the city, plot our route. Gwera and Adridia, I need you to find a library and find out what you can about the dragonslayer. Theal and Faryn, I want you to train with the guards. Befriend them, drink with them. Alcohol inspires loose lips," Jerylia ordered.

"What will you do?" Faryn narrowed his eyes at the princess, implying she was going to do nothing.

"I've made plans to train with Maori. She's promising, much more so than her brother. I think she and I could be friends, had we met under different circumstances. I only wish she would inherit the throne instead of her brother." The princess sipped her wine, the flavor was sweeter than the dry wine made for getting drunk more so than the flavor that was common in Serradon. "I do believe it's time for bed." A weariness had settled over her bones and the constant hum of the earth beneath her was beginning to drive her mad. She could feel the call but any attempt to use her magic was futile, like straining to reach something and just brushing your fingers against the edge. She stood and placed her dirty plate back on the cart before striding over to the bed. The silk sheets were soft as she sunk down on the mattress, her fingers running over the gold detailing in an ocean of blue. Her companions left, all except for Adridia who glanced at the princess with concerned eyes.

"Are you okay, Jerylia?" Her head snapped up. Adridia seldom used her full name. She sighed and pulled back the thin sheets, crawling underneath them, sleep tugging at her eyelids.

"I'm so tired, Adri. I'm tired and my whole body is on edge from the magic of this place," she whispered, her eyelids growing heavy. The bed groaned as the warrior climbed into the bed from the other side.

"It's your magic awakening. It's growing and it's taking its toll. Just rest now, Little Serra." Jerylia's eyelids closed and she fell into sleep.

She was home. Trees rose around her, pillars against the

dark sky. Fog swirled around her ankles and she was alive from the hum of the forest. She could feel it in every inch of her as gooseflesh appeared on her arms. A twig snapped behind her and she whirled. She was not alone. A woman stepped out from behind a thick tree, her white robes brushing the ground. Her hair was the same shade as Jerylia's and two pointed ears poked out from beneath it. Her face was gentle but her blue eyes were fierce. She glowed, breaking apart the darkness surrounding them.

"Who are you?" Jerylia's voice echoed into the forest around them. The woman cocked her head, smiling, revealing elongated canines.

"You already know that." Her voice held centuries and was soft but at the same time, hewn from granite.

"Serra." Jerylia squared her shoulders, looking her ancestor in the eyes.

"I am in your blood, therefore I am in you, allowing you to commune with me here, as you may commune with all your ancestors powerful enough to travel here." The princess shifted, her skin tightening over her bones.

"What's happening?" She closed her eyes against the pain. Serra's eyes flared once.

"You are very important, Jerylia. Every moment in history, every queen descended from me, it all has led to you. Your mother is important as is your father."

"My father? What does he have to do with anything?" The pain was nearly overwhelming and the princess fell to her knees.

"Your father was part dark elf, descended from someone of great importance, though his bloodline was lost to history." Serra pinned the princess with her gaze. "He is in your blood too."

"My father? He barely had any magic."

"Not the Blacksmith of the North."

"Then who?" she screamed, clutching her head in her hands. Serra whipped her head to the right, her eyes finding something in the darkness.

"We're not alone."

The sun filtered through the curtains blowing lazily in the wind as Jerylia bolted up in her bed, fingers clawing at her hair and her breathing heavy. Adridia was awake in an instant, folding Jerylia's hands into her own.

"What happened?" she asked once the princess had levelled out her breathing.

"I met Serra in my dream. She's given me hints about my heritage that I need to solve." Jerylia pulled her hands from Adridia's and padded over to the carved wardrobe.

"The silver one would bring out your eyes." Gwera was leaning against one of the bedposts. Jerylia smiled gratefully before pulling the thin silk dress off the hanger. Her arms were bare and a slit in the skirt of the dress allowed the pale skin of her leg to peek through when she walked.

"I want to explore the city today. Maybe plot an escape route." She propped her bare leg on the edge of the bed and buckled her thigh strap around her thigh, tucking her dagger on the inside.

"You need to slow down for a minute." Gwera gripped her by the shoulders and looked her in the eye. "Ever since we've arrived here you've been acting strange." Jerylia took a deep breath.

"I can feel the magic here in my blood, in my bones. It's driving me mad, Gwera. I have to keep moving and thinking to keep my mind off it." The witch's eyes softened.

"I can make you a tonic. It will put a damper on your magic just until we get home." The princess breathed a sigh of relief.

"Thank you." She squared her shoulders, the strap around her leg snug against her skin. She strode over to the door and opened it, poking her head out to locate a guard.

"Princess Maori offered us a tour yesterday. Could you tell her I'm looking for her?" she asked the guard posted a few feet from her door. He nodded and walked away, his footsteps echoing down the hallway.

The streets of Isef were swollen with elves shopping the mid-day market. Stalls overflowing with decorations and traditional baubles for the festival lined the edges, the people flowing down the middle like the current of a river. The five companions followed the princess closely as she led them through the maze of roads that crossed over each other in what seemed like every direction. Stalls with every good that money could buy drew their attention. One stall even sold exotic pets. Lizards and rare birds sat in cages, their bright colors bringing people in to investigate.

"This is amazing." The princess gazed at the crowd with awe in her eyes. "It reminds me of the preparations we do for Asaydalas back home." Memories of sunny days spent in Asaydil at the summer palace for the summer holiday flashed behind her eyes.

"We have so many festivals throughout the year, you would think the people would grow bored of them." Princess Maori's fire-bright eyes were alight with joy. Jerylia could tell she enjoyed being out among her people instead of stuffed inside her father's palace. Her smile faded as her eyes lifted to the sky and a roar shook the city. Adridia was at Jerylia's side immediately, ready to protect her. A black shadow passed over them. Her mouth dropped open at the sight of the massive wingspan and giant scaled body attached to them.

"T-that's a dragon." She gripped Maori's shoulders and pointed after the flying creature. "They're supposed to be dead."

"I can explain." Her dark eyes searched Jerylia's with no ill intent.

"Then explain it." She became all too aware of the dagger still strapped to her thigh.

"The dragonslayer didn't kill the dragons. He killed their reign of terror. He has the power to speak to them and understand them. He called them all to the northern mountains. He supposedly still lives there. We seldom see them this far south." Jerylia let the foreign princess go and stared at her, trying to unravel the confusion that had knotted itself in her head.

"But the traveler we talked to told us he killed them." Maori shook her head.

"The story has been told so many times, it may have gotten twisted or some locals lied to a merchant to make the story more interesting." She raked her hair back with her fingers. "My father told me the story himself. It happened only a hundred years ago."

"This changes everything," Jerylia whispered, turning to look at Adridia. The warrior nodded, knowing exactly what was going through the princess' mind. In their original plan, they were retrieving one person to help them fight against Sinisstra and her dragons. Now if they were successful, they could potentially return with a whole host of dragons to rival the Draerigean Empress.

Chapter 13

Adridia

The warrior and the witch wandered the endless halls of the royal palace, stopping every so often to ask the guards for directions. The pair received strange looks from servants and other visitors to the palace, as they were opposite in every way possible. Gwera was petite and ladylike, with her long dress that whispered over the floor as they walked, and Adridia was tall and muscle-bound, content to wander the palace in her casual attire.

"How hard could it be to find a goddess-damned library?" Gwera muttered as they passed yet another room that was not what they were searching for. Laughter at the end of the hallway drew their attention. Jerylia and the Hrinthian princess rounded the corner in full Hrinthian armor, hardened leather shells held together by a breathable cloth that left their abdomens exposed, both laden with weapons.

"We'll be in the training yard if you need us," Jerylia said, her lips stretched into an easy smile. The tonic Gwera gave her to dampen her magic was working and she was easing back into normalcy, as normal as she could, at least, with her mother still in Sinisstra's grasp. Adridia was relieved that the princess was feeling better. It would have made this whole mess a lot worse if they'd had to carry her everywhere with them.

"We still haven't found the library. We've been asking the guards but they just led us in circles," Maori chuckled.

"They like to mess with visitors. I'll yell at them for it later. You'll find it three halls to the left. The door is flanked by statues of Della," the princess explained. The witch thanked her before they continued down the hall, following her directions. The doors to the library were carved intricately with many figures depicting different stories from Hrithian lore. Gwera ran her fingers over two women draped in silk dancing together before pushing open the thick wooden door.

Adridia had forgotten how much the witch loved being surrounded by books. The warrior watched as Gwera closed her eyes and breathed in deep through her nose. She then turned to survey the massive library. Shelves lined the walls and spiraled up into the tower. Small areas lined with cushions broke up the otherwise spotless marble floors. A beautiful marble staircase with a twisted iron banister led up to the second floor, curving with the wall of the library. Librarians in thin white robes moved silently through the room, working quietly but efficiently. Jerylia had told them that the librarians here were treated almost like priestesses because they protected knowledge, something Hrinthians held in the highest regard.

"It's going to be impossible to find what we're looking for," she grumbled under her breath, irritation grinding at her stomach.

"I can help with that." The witch grinned, closing her eyes once again. Her slim fingers twisted in front of her, thin green wisps of magic slipping from under her nails. Adridia would never tire of watching the witch weave her magic. Her hands moved in ways that were almost hypnotizing and the green magic was beautiful as it gathered around her fingers. The magic whisked away, weaving through the shelves and in between books until Gwera's eyes snapped open. "Top floor."

The warrior groaned, glaring at the stairs like an enemy she could vanquish. "That's a lot of floors," she grumbled as they began climbing the steps, their silk slippers soundless on the marble floor.

The books they were searching for were hand-bound, messily, as if done in a hurry. Twine stuck out the tops of the binding and the leather was cracked. Adridia drew one from the shelf and opened it, running her fingers over the handwritten words, the script sloppy and uneven. Gwera bundled them into her arms and claimed a small cushioned area, folding her legs underneath her like a lady. Adridia snorted and sprawled across the pillows, taking up as much space as possible. She opened a book and let it rest on her stomach, the two women falling into a comfortable silence.

"Are you content?" Adridia was the first to break the silence, the warrior never comfortable in complete silence.

"What's that supposed to mean?" The witch didn't sound offended, just confused.

"Are you content as you are? Never mating, without a partner," the warrior clarified. The witch laughed and shook her head, smiling slightly.

"Of course I am content. I became accustomed to the idea of being alone long ago. I learned to love myself enough for any mate that would come my way so that I would not need one, not for any of the eight hundred years I hope to live," Gwera explained.

"But what if you unexpectedly found one?" Her curiosity was getting the better of her.

"I don't think that's likely to happen."

"Why not?"

"Because I figured out a long time ago that I am not attracted to males and the females that are attracted to females, do not find me attractive." Adridia's heart softened. She'd had her trysts with both males and females and found them both enjoyable but the one elf she was absolutely enamored by was a male. Gwera looked up from her book and smiled at the warrior.

"Do not be sad for me. If Eowessa wishes for me to have a mate, I will find one. Until then, I am happy to be alone." She focused her attention back on the book in her lap.

"You're never going to be alone, Gwere. You'll always have the squadron." Gwera glanced up and gave Adridia a warm smile before flipping a yellowing page. The warrior looked back down at her book, her leg shaking up and down as she tried to concentrate. She squeezed her eyes shut as the letters on the page began to swirl together. She already had a difficult time reading and this curling script was making it worse.

"Stop doing that." The witch didn't even look up from her book.

"Stop doing what?"

"Bouncing your leg. You know it makes me crazy."

"I can't concentrate unless a part of me is moving."

"Your heart is moving as it beats, isn't that enough?" Adridia snorted and pinned the smaller elf with an incredulous look.

"Not all of us were born to let magic do everything for us. I have a strong connection to water. I need to move, be flowing, or else I grow stagnant."

"Grow stagnant," Gwera deadpanned. Adridia sighed and stopped bouncing her leg.

Her eyes were soon wandering the room, looking for anything else except for her book.

"Find anything?" Adridia asked, her fingers tapping on the cover of the book in her lap.

"Not anything we didn't already know. You could help me

find something, then you could go train with Jerylia and Maori."

"That sounds like heaven." They both sat in silence for a while longer before Gwera breathed deeply like she was going to say something then chose not to. Adridia just raised an eyebrow at her, happy to have a reason not to be staring at the moving words anymore.

"Can I ask you a question?" she finally spoke.

"I'm pretty sure you're going to ask me anyway."

"Do you know how he feels about you?" Adridia looked up from her book in shock.

"Who?" Of course, the warrior already knew who the witch spoke of, she just wanted her to say it out loud. Gwera snorted.

"You know who." She stuck her finger in between the pages of her book and leaned forward, glaring at the warrior. "Theal," Adridia sighed.

"Yes, I'm aware of his feelings," the witch sighed.

"And what are your feelings?"

"He's a handsome elf."

"That's it?"

"What else do you want me to say, Gwera? That I'm in love with him?"

"I'm just curious. C'mon, I answered your questions." Adridia sighed and met the witch's gaze.

"Ever since I discovered his affections for me, I've let myself wonder. Yes, I'm attracted to him, maybe I even love him in a romantic way, but I fear what a relationship could do to our friendship, to the squadron, if it ended poorly. I never wanted to put Jerylia into a position where she would have to choose between us. She's known him since childhood, he's like a brother to her and she's my best friend," she explained. Gwera's eyes softened.

"But he could also be your best chance at successful mateship. I know you fear what could happen if it ends badly but that is an 'if'. If he cares for you and you care for him, don't fight it." Gwera reached out and squeezed Adridia's hand. "Your heart is a compass, it could never lead you astray."

"Thank you, Gwera." Her lips turned upwards in a soft smile before they both turned back to their books. They sat, submerged in silence for a long while before Gwera broke it.

"Oh my Goddess, Adri, look." She showed the warrior the page she had been reading. Her eyes scanned the page quickly even as the letters blended together. She let out a breath she had been holding.

"We have to go tell Jerylia."

The two elves were nearly tripping over their slippers as they emerged into the courtyard. Sparring soldiers halted, blades mid-air to watch the red-faced northerners sprint across the dusty cobblestones. The princess leaned on a training dummy as they approached, sweat gleaming on her exposed skin.

"You two look as if you're aching to tell me something." She let out a breathy laugh.

"We found these journals—"

"He lives in the mountains—" Both elves started speaking at the same time.

"Stop!" The princess held up both her hands and they silenced themselves. "One of you speak." Adridia glanced at Gwera and nodded.

"He lives in Greydell."

"That sounds like a Serradonian name. Is that all you found?"

"It's in the mountains in the northernmost part of Hrinth and it's not written on any maps because the Hrinthians don't consider it a real city. It's just the dragonslayer there with his dragons. It's an ancient castle that was abandoned during the Great War almost three thousand years ago," Gwera explained.

"So he saves them from the dragons and they repay him by pretending he doesn't exist. I see why he's so secluded," Jerylia scoffed.

"They also don't want anyone to find him because he's the only thing keeping the dragons at bay. As long as he's alive, the dragons don't bother the people," Adridia interjected.

"Those journals didn't happen to reveal his name, did they?" The princess pulled at the leather tie holding her hair back, allowing it to fall around her face.

"His name is Caerin Ocealith."

"So how do we find a man that doesn't want to be found?"

"We have to speak with Sevag at the Ishtuk's Beak in Djat. The information we got in Kher was at least right about one thing. He can tell us where to find him, or at the very least where to start looking," Gwera finished.

"So that leaves us with only one problem."

"What problem?"

Jerylia leaned in close so no one would overhear them. "How to escape this fucking palace."

Chapter 14

Jerylia

The princess of Serradon woke to someone singing, loudly, in the bathing room next door. She groaned and rolled over in the silk sheets, covering her pointed ears with the pillow. Soft footsteps surrounded her and then the sheets were pulled away from her body.

"No!" she whined and curled up on herself. The servants began babbling in Hrinthian. Jerylia huffed and sat up, rubbing her eyes with the heels of her hands. The servants glanced up and began giggling. "I get it, my hair looks like an ishtuk nest." She snapped in Hrinthian, before slipping out of the bed and padding down the hall to the bathing room.

"Gwera, there are other people in this hallway who enjoy their sleep," she grumbled as she stripped out of her nightclothes.

"You don't get to lecture me when you're walking around with that hair." Jerylia scowled as she slipped into the foaming pool.

"I forgot how much you enjoy festivals and balls," the princess commented as she tilted her head back to wet her hair. Her servants began tugging at it, brushing through the knots.

"Stop yelling at me! I don't know what you're saying!" Adridia stumbled into the bathing room, sleep dragging her limbs. Her servants just ignored her yelling and continued speaking to her, pulling at her clothes.

"Just get in the tub," Jerylia said, closing her eyes as the elves massaged shampoo into her scalp. "Don't bother fighting them, it won't work."

"I am one of the most feared warriors in all of Serradon. They can't just drag me around and make me look pretty. I was not made to be pretty." She hissed through her teeth as she undressed and slid into the pool.

"The sooner you cooperate, the sooner we can leave," Gwera sang. Adridia just grumbled as the servants went to work on her.

"Good morning, ladies." Jerylia jerked her head up as Faryn's deep baritone echoed around the chamber. Adridia wrinkled her nose as she glanced at him.

"What are you two doing here?" Gwera asked.

"We all share this bathing chamber. The one in the other hall that we used before was being used," he said as he began pulling off his clothes. Jerylia looked down at her hands underneath the surface of the water as the twins slid into the pool. The servants yanked on her hair, her head whipping back. The soap foam covered most of their bodies, preserving the princess' modesty. Theal was avoiding eye contact with everybody, his cheeks flaming red.

"Theal, how many women have you bedded and a simple bath has you redder than my hair." Gwera was chuckling as a servant lifted her arm and began shaving the hair from it. Several servants had entered the pool to ensure that the females were hairless from top to bottom.

"The only person allowed to see the princess naked is her consort," Theal said in a low tone, his eyes darting towards Adridia.

"We are not in Serradon, my dear archer. Hrinthians feel no shame in the elven body. They celebrate their lack of modesty.

They don't understand our rules and traditions," she chided, her voice melodic.

"We aren't Hrinthian, are we, Gwera," Faryn snapped, his dark locks swaying in front of his eyes.

"He's right, Gwere. If we abandon our traditions, we are no longer Serradonian," Jerylia spoke up. The witch sucked in a breath before standing, water running down her body in rivulets, her tattoos stark against her pale skin. The twins looked away quickly. The servants wrapped her in a silk robe before leading her out of the bath chamber.

"Your turn, Princess," the servant who had washed her hair told her in Hrinthian.

"Turn away," she said to her comrades. "Have the robe ready, please. They are not allowed to see me…" The princess paused as she spoke to the servant. There was no Hrithian word for naked, for they felt no shame from it. "…Skin," she finished, gesturing to her torso area. The servant nodded in understanding and prepared the robe, holding it open for Jerylia to don as soon as she stepped out of the water.

Back in her room, the servants tugged at her hair and pinched at her skin. The princess felt like a doll, being prepared and dressed for a display. They combed her hair until it was dry, making sure the locks were pin-straight as they fell around her shoulders. A chain with blue jewels was wrapped around her head, pinned in her hair, so the large pendant in the front sat in the middle of her forehead. They forced her into a dress with fish scales sewn into the bodice so she shimmered in the lights. They painted her face with a silver iridescent powder, so her cheekbones and nose shone when she turned her head.

The festivities were in full swing by the time they made their way down to the feast hall. The smell of smoked fish filled the air. Dancers wearing only painted patterns of fish scales performed throughout the room. In the corner, a small band played a jaunty tune with woodwinds. Gwera was smiling, her massive amounts of hair piled in coils on top of her head.

"You know the plan?" the princess asked the rest of them, without turning towards them. The Hrinthian princess had already spotted them and had begun making her way towards them.

"Of course," Gwera purred and in an instant, her entire demeanor changed as she snatched a goblet of wine off a servant's tray. Her body loosened as she danced towards the guards standing at attention along the walls, offering them spelled wine.

"Princess!" Maori greeted Jerylia, grabbing her wrists. "Come, my father would like you to dine with us tonight," she began dragging her away.

"Wait." Jerylia paused, glancing back at Adridia. "Will my personal guard be allowed at the royal table?"

"Why do you have a royal guard, warrior princess?"

"My mother is, well she was, a bit overprotective. She wanted to make sure I had adequate protection, even though I am very much capable of protecting myself." Maori glanced behind her at the tall blonde, who tugged at her tight bodice. In truth, the princess just didn't want to be left alone with the foreign royals. Prince Griel made her skin crawl with distrust and the king intimidated her with his age.

"Of course she can join us." The princess and the warrior followed Maori to the royal table, where the ancient king greeted them with a respectful nod.

"I hear you're a great warrior in your land." The prince leaned back in his seat and jutted his chin out, almost challenging.

"The queens of Serradon are raised to be warriors. It would bring shame upon the royal line if I were not a great warrior." Jerylia leaned forward, her forearms resting against the edge of the table.

"Then entertain us with one of your stories. People always tell the same stories at all of these functions and they grow rather boring." Something glinted in his eyes, a challenge to her claim of heroism.

"There was once a huge slaving operation in one of our border cities. Slavers would kidnap people from all over Serradon and cross the border into the southern countries to get to Draerige. The dark elves use forest and mountain elves as slaves, though they prefer mountain elves because of the magic in our blood. The forest elves they use for hard physical labor, oftentimes it's the thing that kills them. They believe they are beneath them because they wield no magic. It's one of the many things that have put us on the brink of war with Draerige before."

"How old were you when we took down that operation?" Adridia asked.

"I was only nineteen. I could still barely hold a sword. I used two weighted daggers instead but it meant I had to get close to my enemies in order to kill them."

"We snuck into their camp at night, just the small squadron to make the element of surprise more effective. Jerylia and I still didn't get along well. It wasn't until she took an arrow that was meant for me that we began to trust each other."

"I remember that. We lost the element of surprise because we couldn't stop bickering."

"Luckily the slavers weren't very prepared for a fight. They had grown comfortable and were lured into a false sense of security. They had a huge shipment they were preparing for transport and we couldn't let them get away."

"I saw one of them aiming an arrow at Adridia's throat. I leapt in front of her and the arrow struck me in the shoulder. We killed almost all of the slavers and the rest we put in the slave cages and hauled back to Serramor for questioning," Jerylia finished. "The would-be slaves went home to their families. Unfortunately, a similar operation not far from there that we had planned to hit later ended up moving out early because of our attack. If we had brought a larger attack force, we could have saved both camps but my stubbornness cost those elves their freedom."

"If I may interrupt." The royals glanced up to see Theal standing at the end of the table, his hands folded gently behind his back. "I would like to ask Adridia for a dance." Jerylia nodded when the warrior glanced at her in question. She stood and took his hand, following him to the open space in front of the band.

"Did you find the leader of the operation?" Maori asked.

"We did. My mother questioned him herself. He lasted longer than I thought he would. It took twelve days for him to break. Bless my mother, she was able to find the locations of all the other operation leaders in Serradon."

"But Draerige still uses slaves." The princess nodded solemnly.

"They do. My mother visited Empress Ceanna and begged her to stop slavery in Draerige but the empress refused. She said slavery was no worse than the slums of Serradon. That many of the slaves in Draerige are treated well and have opportunities to earn better jobs or even their freedom. In the slums of Serradon, there is almost no way out, that our people are stuck living in squalor, working themselves to the bone just to afford food. It's because of that conversation that my mother implemented charity programs all throughout Serradon, shelters, and kitchens to supply food for elves who can't afford it. There are even programs to help elves without jobs find and keep one. The nobles of Serradon weren't thrilled when we asked them to give away their money but once the queen insisted they would be paving the way for a better future for Serradon, they were eager to donate."

"I thought there had been peace in Cordava for thousands of years," the prince eagerly jumped into the conversation.

"There has been but things have been tenuous with Draerige for a while. Neither ruler has done anything about it because we've all been too afraid of war," Jerylia explained.

"You young rulers are too paralyzed by the fear of starting a war to successfully rule." The king spoke. "You cannot claim to know what is best for your people when you are afraid of what may happen if you defend them." He leaned forward and stared at Jerylia with eyes clouded with age. "What happened to the Serradonians sold into slavery in Draerige?" he asked.

"I don't know. I begged my mother to allow me to go rescue them but she forbade me from ever stepping foot in Draerige." He pointed a crooked finger at Jerylia.

"Her fear clouded her judgment. I have not been a perfect king but I hope that my children learn from my mistakes." He sat back in his chair, a rough cough escaping his lips. The prince nodded solemnly, his mate still silent beside him.

Jerylia caught Gwera's eye across the room. The witch nodded, a goblet of wine hanging loosely in her hand. The princess smiled to herself as she surveyed the rest of the room. Theal and Adridia were dancing, his hands loose on her hips but his back tight with tension, as if he was nervous. Adridia was looking anywhere but at the elf in front of her. Faryn was draped against the wall, a woman in his arms. The princess raised her glass to her lips and downed the contents, heat rushing to her stomach.

The palace was quiet, stars winking in the dark sky above them. Jerylia's sandals made soft clicking on the marble floors as she, along with her companions, sneaked through the open halls. Her clothes whispered from the movement as they passed into the garden, the cool night air greeting her warm cheeks.

"They keep the ishtuks in the back of the stables, near the west entrance of the gardens," Gwera whispered as they passed through a forest of cacti.

"You should also try to be quieter when you're trying to sneak out of my palace." Panic shot through Jerylia as a voice spoke from behind them. They all turned to face the Hrinthian princess.

"Maori," Jerylia breathed. Her hand crept towards the sword sheathed at her hip. Maori's hand shot out and Jerylia's surroundings melted away. She was in a mountain forest, snow under her feet, but the air was still warm around her. Her mouth fell open and her hand fell away from her sword as she allowed the sounds of the mountain forest to swallow her. Her heart clenched in her chest as she thought of home. "What is this?"

"Della gave me the power to conjure mirages." The Princess lowered her hand and the scene melted back into the royal gardens.

"Maori, you have to let us go. Sinisstra has my mother. I have no idea what's happening in my own country," Jerylia pleaded, tears springing to her eyes. "The dragonslayer is the only one who can help me."

"Of course I'm going to let you leave." Relief swelled in her chest at those words.

She reached out and pulled the foreign princess into a tight hug.

"Thank you."

"My father did not keep you here out of malice. He only wanted to make sure no Hrinthian would harm you but since you are leaving he will feel betrayed and try to contact Sinisstra. I will work to convince him not to send for the empress. Hrinth will back you in this fight if I have any say in it."

"What about your brother?" Adridia asked from behind the princess.

"Griel will be a problem but not one that I can't handle." Maori pulled back and squeezed Jerylia's hand. "Now, go. You should hurry. The guards will be starting the before-dawn rounds soon." She turned and headed back into the palace while the six companions escaped under the vigilant eyes of both pale moons, racing towards the horizon.

Chapter 15

Jerylia

The sun beat down on them as they travelled across the sand. The ishtuks smelled like hot livestock beneath them. Jerylia's skin had turned red and began to blister. They had run out of water during the first day of travel. She could feel death looming over them but she refused to go out this way. This could not be their end.

"Gwera, how much longer?" Her voice was rough.

"We should be there just after nightfall." The princess shuddered as she thought back to the night before with the five of them huddled together to stay warm. The desert was the place of extremes, extreme heat during the day and extreme cold during the night. They hadn't been able to find fuel for a fire and had ended up sleeping piled together.

"Why does Della hate us?" Adridia moaned from atop her bird, her eyes closed against the sun.

"Della doesn't care about us. It's this goddess-forsaken desert. There's a reason the legends call it a living entity, an unkillable monster that enjoys killing travelers." Gwera glared down at the sand as if she could strike it down like she would a foe.

The day dragged on and eventually, the sun dipped below the horizon and the twin moons rose behind them. Djat was a small town built on an oasis fed by an underground spring. Two massive palm trees stood guard at the entrance to the settlement. The six companions abandoned their ishtuks when they entered and dragged themselves to the first inn they saw. The man behind the counter took them in with wide eyes as they paid for a room and ordered water to be brought to them. The door had barely shut before the princess passed out on the broken sofa across from the bed.

She was in the forest again, mist swirling around her ankles. She was alone, or at least she thought she was. The trees around her called out to her, their collective voices rising in a choir.

"You're ignoring yourself, little goddess." Jerylia whirled to find Serra standing there, serene as always. She was perfect, glowing, radiant.

"What did you mean last time we spoke? Who was here? What did he have to do with my father?" She stepped forward, merely a foot away from the princess. Jerylia had to tilt her head up to look her in the face.

"Only your most powerful ancestors can meet you in this place. You are descended from me through your mother and the queens' line."

"I've heard the song of the earth. If I was descended from another god through my father, wouldn't I hear another call?" She arched an eyebrow.

"He is buried in your line. You have to draw him out." Her hands lashed out and she seized the princess by the shoulders, her calm composure broken.

"Who is he?" Jerylia screamed, the question echoing around them.

"I am life." She was no longer in front of the princess. She whirled to see Serra facing away from her. She turned to face the princess, her elongated canines bared, ivy crawling over her

cheekbones and across her forehead. It swallowed her until she was nothing but a writhing mass of greenery. "He is destruction." She was suddenly behind Jerylia, whispering in her ear. She jumped away from the goddess.

"Stop speaking in riddles." The princess clutched her head with clawed fingers. The green column grew larger. Serra's head whipped around and she stared at something behind it. The leaves turned black as flames engulfed the column. She shielded her eyes from the light and the heat but then Serra was behind her again, her hands gripping her head, forcing her to look at it.

"See what he does. I create life and he can destroy it with a single thought," she hissed in Jerylia's ear.

"Who are you?" the princess screamed at the fire.

"I am you." A dark elf loomed over her. His dark grey skin was set aglow by the diadem of flames set on his brow. He was a stranger, every piece of him foreign, except for his eyes.

His eyes were her father's.

The princess gasped awake, disturbing the water she was submerged in. She blinked a few times, gathering in her surroundings. She was in some kind of underground chamber. Tubs were carved into the stone floor and women draped in white shifts walked barefoot between the numerous rows of them. This seemed to be a place of healing for elves who got trapped in the desert. She glanced down at herself. Her skin was still an unnaturally bright red from exposure to the sun but the blisters were gone and she had been hydrated somehow. Her tongue no longer felt like sand in her mouth. One older woman noticed her and rushed over, a folded towel in her arms.

"Where are my friends?" she asked the woman.

"One with red hair brought you here. They wait for you at Ishtuk's Beak," the servant told her in broken Serradonian.

Jerylia bolted out of the water, snatching the towel from the woman.

"Clothes?" she asked and was handed a thin white shift that matched the ones the servants wore. "Thank you so much for your kindness." The woman nodded and moved on to other patrons of the underground bathhouse.

The streets of the oasis town were busy, dust clouding the air from the foot traffic. The tavern seemed to be at the center of all the activity, drunks stumbling from the open doorway. The princess ducked inside, narrowly missing an obese man vomiting on the crumbling porch. She wrinkled her nose and moved on, her keen eyes searching for her companions.

"Long live the queen!" Theal exclaimed as she sat down at a crooked table with them.

"I am not the queen yet." Her voice cracked as she spoke.

"My statement still stands. I wish your mother a very long life." Jerylia gave him a soft smile before searching the rest of the tavern.

"Have you made contact with Sevag?" she asked.

"No, we were waiting for you," Gwera replied, pulling her clean shift tighter around her as she eyed the filthy establishment.

"Thank you for getting me to the bathhouse." The princess was quiet for another moment. "I had another dream about Serra."

"What did the almighty goddess have to say this time?" Adridia asked even though she was looking anywhere but at the people sitting around the table. Her eyes were flicking between the other tavern patrons and the door, her hand on her sword.

"She wasn't alone. She told me only my most powerful ancestors could meet me in my dreams and that my father was descended from someone very powerful." Jerylia folded her hands together. "He appeared." Gwera was leaning forward, staring at her in anticipation. "He's a dark elf, one who controls fire."

"Could it be possible that he's one of the Draerigian gods? They're the only country that worships the dark fae," Gwera said, her eyes wide.

"I think it's very possible," the princess replied. Their conversation was interrupted by a barmaid walking up to their table, inquiring about their dinner.

"I will take the biggest bowl you have of that amazing stew I smell cooking in the back," Adridia told her. She nodded and glanced at the rest of them, her eyes catching on Faryn draped in his chair, a flirtatious smirk on his lips. Jerylia rolled her eyes and ordered herself a bowl of stew as well, her stomach rumbling at the thought of food.

"I would also like to inquire about a man who is known to frequent this establishment. His name is Sevag." The barmaid's eyes lit up in recognition.

"Let me guess, he owes you money?" Jerylia glanced at her companions.

"Something like that." She gave the barmaid a tight smile.

"He sits in the corner every night and drinks himself into a stupor before stumbling home before the lizards wake." She jerked her thumb to a small round table in the corner with a short scruff of a man collapsed on top of it.

"Fucking perfect," Theal muttered. Jerylia was inclined to agree with him. Hopefully, Sevag was lucid enough to point them in the right direction of Greydell.

"Gwera, you're with me." Jerylia stood. "Boys, please make sure Adri doesn't drown herself in that stew and make sure she doesn't eat mine or someone is going to lose an ear."

"Jer, we know better than to get between Adridia and food." Faryn nursed his warm ale, grimacing after he swallowed.

"She broke my finger, Jer." Theal folded his arms over his chest. Adridia slammed her palm down on the table.

"It was your pinkie and I said I was sorry." She pointed an accusatory finger across the table at him.

"All I did was take a potato off your plate! A potato!"

"And you never did it again, did you?" Jerylia and Gwera shared a wary glance.

"Maybe this argument can wait until later." Adridia slouched in her chair grumbling while Theal started speaking quietly with his twin. Jerylia rolled her eyes and straightened her spine, preparing herself to speak with Sevag. Gwera was at her hip as she marched up to the snoring sack of flesh in the corner.

"Sevag?" She kicked the leg of the table, shaking it underneath him. His breathing hitched and he sat up abruptly, drool dripping off his chin. He blinked a few times, his eyes finding the two women in front of him.

"Can I help you?" His fingers found the tin cup still sitting on the table and he brought it to his lips.

"I was told you know where to find Greydell, where the dragonslayer lives. His name is—" He cut her off.

"I know what his name is." He drank deeply from his cup, loosing a loud belch before speaking again. "You need to go to Rert. There's a tavern there, called the Shrieking Cactus. Talk to Vael. He can help you." A flash of irritation speared through the princess.

"And why can't you just tell me how to get to Greydell?" She leaned forward and laid her palms flat on the wooden table, the surface sticky with old drink.

"Because Caerin declined to tell me where it is. Didn't trust me with that information," he chuckled, the sound echoing into his cup as he prepared to take another drink. "Can't imagine why." He set his cup back down on the table and met her glare. "Look, I told you everything he told me. He said if anyone ever came asking after him, to send them to Rert."

"Enjoy your evening." The words were pleasant but filled with venom as the princess turned and stalked away from the table.

"Where are we going?" Adridia spoke around a mouthful of stew as they returned to the table.

"Rert. We have to find Vael at the Shrieking Cactus."

"Great Serra's tits," Faryn grumbled. "Another trip across the desert."

"Let's not pass out from sun sickness this time," Theal suggested.

"That was going to be the first step of the plan," Jerylia quipped as she dug into her own bowl of stew. Weariness was already beginning to set in and she had a feeling nothing about this journey was going to be easy.

Chapter 16

Gwera

The tattoos that wrapped around her arms and legs hummed with magical energy. The witch closed her eyes against the sun, turning her face towards it. The sweeping sands of the desert shifted with the wind blowing unhindered across it. Her companions were laughing and belting out Serradonian war songs. She smiled at her friends, rotating her wrists to keep the air flowing around them to prevent sun sickness.

"So watch your back because the warrior queens of Serradon will put a dagger in your ribs." Adridia finished the song with a dramatic jab in front of her, the ishtuk underneath her ruffling its feathers as she became unbalanced.

"I will pay you to stop singing." Faryn gripped a thick rope in his free hand, a lead on Theal's ishtuk which carried their supplies while he flew above them in his eagle form. Occasionally he would swoop down and weave in between their ishtuks, letting out excited chirps.

"I seem to remember you singing that particular song at the last victory celebration we had before we set our sights on the King of Thieves. And I remember you butchering every note." The warrior adjusted the thin scarf wrapped around her head, securing it so her face was shadowed.

"All I remember from that night were the two beautiful women I bedded." He lifted his chin in pride.

"Faryn, I feel that enough time has passed for me to tell you this. One of those women ended up in my bed and boy did she have a lot to say about your performance." The archer's eyes glinted as he glared at the warrior.

"Did she use the word 'godlike'?" Faryn smirked and puffed out his chest.

"She didn't use that word but she did compare us if you would like to hear the results. It was a number-based system if I recall correctly. I scored a five while you scored a mere one."

"Well, what were the numbers based on?" Adridia grinned, teeth flashing in the sun.

"Orgasms." Faryn scowled and faced forward, having been beaten in their small battle of wits.

"None of that changes the fact that the two least musically inclined people in our group should not be arguing about which one of them should be singing," Jerylia spoke up. "Because the answer is, neither of you should be singing." The eagle above them whistled in agreement. Faryn frowned on his ishtuk. In a flash of golden light, he was soaring next to Theal, the twin birds chasing each other over the sands. They both had beautiful golden feathers with patches of black tipping their wings, curved beaks glinting in the sunlight. Theal's left wing had a soft white streak across the middle from when he had broken his arm in a fight, his animal form permanently altered.

"Have you had any more of those dreams?" Gwera pulled her bird up beside the Princess.

"Serra has not shown herself to me." Jerylia had done a good job of appearing in good spirits but the tattoos on Gwera's left arm strengthened her connection to the mind. They allowed her to feel the impression of the thoughts in someone's head, to know the emotions they're feeling, no matter how well they may hide them. A sweep of her fingers told her everything she needed to know about what was going through her friend's mind. The princess was at war with herself. She was worried about the Queen and puzzled over Serra's messages.

"Have you been able to use your powers yet?" She knew the princess had been feeling the connection to the life around her but had not yet attempted to control it. She was sympathetic towards the princess. It had taken her so long to realize her own powers and Jerylia's were right there in front of her yet still out of her reach.

"I haven't even tried." She glanced at Adridia who was swatting at the raptors now snapping at her clothes. "I'm afraid to. What if I try to call life but instead receive destruction?" Gwera's eyes softened. The princess was so young compared to her elders. Gwera herself was only forty-three, aged by her experiences.

"Your powers are still new. You will grow comfortable with whatever power presents itself when it's time." They both turned their attention to Adridia as she shrieked in frustration, the twins whistling to each other. Gwera rolled her eyes and held out her arm. Theal was careful with his talons as he landed gracefully on the outstretched limb. He lifted a wing and preened his feathers with his curved beak. Faryn landed on Jerylia's shoulder, the princess hissing when his talons pierced her skin.

"No armor," she said through gritted teeth. The eagle bumped the top of his head against her cheek in apology before lifting himself off her shoulder. Theal took to the air as well, shifting back to elf form and landing gracefully on Faryn's ishtuk.

"Nightfall is on the horizon." Gwera followed his gaze to the east where the twin moons were peering over the sand. "There's a small cluster of cacti about an hour ahead of us. We'll be more protected from the elements if we make camp there."

"I'm just ready to lay down." Gwera arched her back, her muscles aching in protest. Sweat was beading along the ridges of her back, the constant strain of keeping the wind flowing beginning to take its toll.

"The princess hasn't been resting well." They glanced over at Jerylia who was laughing at Adridia. The warrior was trying to summon enough water from the air to hit Faryn, who dodged every time. "She sleeps but she doesn't rest." The archer shook his head.

"She's worried about her mother. Who knows what kind of horrors the queen has been enduring at the hands of Sinisstra?" Gwera shivered at the thought of her queen, the woman whom she swore to protect at all costs, behind enemy lines.

"What the fuck!" Jerylia screamed and covered her ears, ducking over the thin neck of her ishtuk. Adridia drew her sword, ready to fight any threat to her princess.

"What's wrong?" Gwera and Theal raced over as soon as she screamed. Faryn was chirping and clicking his beak as he swooped around them.

"I heard him. Faryn." Jerylia was still curled in on herself but her hands were no longer covering her ears.

"Yeah, he's being annoying." Adridia swatted at the bird.

"No, I heard him in my head." Faryn finally went quiet. "It was like there was an invisible thread connecting us. I couldn't see it but I could feel that it was there and my mind just latched onto it. After that, I could hear his voice in my head. I'm sorry, I didn't mean to scare you, it just freaked me out."

"Is there a thread between Theal and you?" Gwera asked.

"No, just with Faryn right now," she answered, her knuckles

white as she gripped the leather reigns around her ishtuk's neck.

"Theal, can you shift?" The archer nodded and shifted once more, his talons digging into the soft saddle beneath him. Jerylia gasped.

"Not even my mother could do this." Theal shifted back in a flash of golden light. "She can control greenery and she is able to calm most small animals but she has never been able to speak to them. Only Serra could do that."

"Part of it could be their human soul. Ancient accounts claim Serra could only commune with the most intelligent of animals."

"Perhaps that means my dreams of her were only dreams." The princess curled her fingers in her lap as if she could see the power of life in her palms.

Their gazes were all ripped from the princess when Faryn let out a screech above them. He soared forward and their eyes followed him towards the cluster of cacti not far in front of them. Gwera breathed a sigh of relief, allowing her grip on the wind to slip. The heat from the setting sun rushed over them, quickly cooling as shadows grew longer over the sand. They all made quick work of unloading their bags before lighting a small fire in the center of their circle of bedrolls. Dead cacti burned easily despite the liquid usually kept in the hollow center. They ate a meagre dinner of cooked desert rabbit and stale bread from their packs.

"Do you remember when we had to camp in that bog on the border of Saeroc?" Faryn asked from his position on his bedroll. He had his arms folded above his head, his expression the definition of relaxed.

"Oh, Goddess. I'd rather spend a week in the middle of the desert than camp in that bog again." Adridia shook her head at the memory.

"As if the biting insects weren't bad enough, there was also the smell," Jerylia gagged.

"I spent the entire night at the mess pit we had dug, heaving my guts up," Theal chuckled.

"I'll take the first watch—" Gwera sat up and arched her back, the muscles twitching as she stretched.

"Absolutely not. You don't get a watch because you've spent the entire day conjuring wind around us," Adridia cut her off.

"Adri's right. Sleep until dawn. We can handle it." Gwera only nodded in agreement because sleep was pulling at her eyelids. She tucked herself into her bedroll and let her eyes shut, dreams sweeping her away.

She woke just before dawn, the sun peaking over the horizon. The ground was vibrating. It was a soft thing at first, her magic only picked it up because nothing had made the ground feel like that all night. She sat up and rubbed at her tired eyes, sweeping her hair back, before scanning the desert for trouble. Jerylia had been on watch and was already strapping herself into the set of Hrinthian armor the Hrinthian princess had gifted her. The princess drew her sword from its scabbard, the sound drawing their companions awake. Adridia was on her feet instantly, her greatsword drawn and held in front of her with two hands. The twins were slinging their quivers over their backs and nocking arrows, acute eyes focused on the cloud of dust gradually growing closer. Gwera herself was ready, spells drawn to the tip of her tongue to be whispered in the heat of battle. Green wisps of magic darted in the air around her. She flexed her fingers, preparing herself for the twisting movements she would have to perform.

"It's the Hrinthian guard. No doubt sent after us by the king and his snake of a son." Jerylia hissed through her teeth.

"Hrinthian fighting style is very fluid. Try to break their pattern and they will falter." Gwera took a deep breath in, forcing her mind to calm. A chaotic mind caused chaotic magic, something they couldn't afford right now. The ishtuks' clawed feet sprayed sand as they nearly slid to a stop between two cacti. There had to be at least a dozen of them.

"Princess Jerylia, we were sent to bring you back to the king, through whatever force necessary." The guard in front spoke.

"Good fucking luck." She ground out before her wrist flicked and her dagger lodged in the throat of the guard who had spoken. The woman behind him let out a guttural screech before leaping off of her ishtuk, aiming for the princess. Gwera turned her attention to the rest of the company, her lips moving as she stole the breath from the lungs of one guard, then boiled the blood of the guard behind him. Her magic found a foreign body in the brain of another, fingers forming a 'T' then twisting and curling to make the tumor grow, the guard fell to the ground as he convulsed. A small woman at the back of the company caught her attention. The woman bore no weapons and her fingers moved in unnatural ways, so similar to her own. She watched for a moment in fascination as red streaks of magic swirled around her in a shield. They had sent a witch so she might be challenged, but Gwera only smirked as she planted her feet, squared her shoulders. Her magic wrapped around the witch, feeling for a weakness. There! The witch had anchored her shield at the base of her spine, leaving the spot exposed. A green wisp of magic slithered into the woman's body, crawling up her spine, wreaking havoc as it went. The woman's body contorted, the torso twisting all the way around before she fell into the sand, fingers still twitching.

A shout drew Gwera's attention from behind her and she

whirled, already throwing her magic at her attacker. The guard's eyes popped in his skull and dripped down his face as he screamed. He leaped forward in one last blind attempt to fulfil his mission, his sword slicing the inside of Gwera's thigh. She screamed and fell to her knees, blood flowing over the pale skin. Faryn was at her side in a moment, pulling her into his arms to carry her to the ishtuks. She felt the blood flowing out of her fast, too fast. The bastard had nicked an artery. She recalled a silent spell, one she could weave before she passed out to heal the wound quickly but she needed an ingredient. Her eyes focused on the shifter carrying her.

"Faryn," she moaned in pain, his eyes flicked to her. In a flash, she grabbed the back of his head and slammed her lips to his, her tongue sweeping the inside of his mouth. She pulled back, the spell already moving on her lips.

"Gwera, no." She winked at him before darkness filled her head.

Chapter 17

Jerylia

Jerylia sat by a window, her eyes scanning the street beneath her. Faryn had gone out the day before in eagle form and had returned saying he saw a group of royal soldiers riding into the town. Hrinthian inns had strict privacy rules to protect nobles that might have unseemly company but they couldn't sit in this tiny room forever. Jerylia dragged her eyes from the thin glass to the witch laying in the bed across the room. Her eyes were closed but her lips moved slightly, forming words that none of them could hear.

"This is fucking pointless," Adridia groaned from her chair next to the bed. "I've checked her wound, she's slowly healing. I don't know what she did but it's working. The only thing we can do is wait for her to wake up."

"What else can we do besides wait? There are royal soldiers here, we can't just stroll down the road," Theal countered. Tension was beginning to fill the room. The two had been arguing for the last two days. Jerylia knew it was unresolved feelings between the two creating friction. She nearly rolled her eyes at her two stubborn friends. She couldn't leave them cooped up in this room any longer.

"Theal and I can go to the Shrieking Cactus and meet with Vael. Hopefully, he can send us to Greydell, or I might have to stab someone." Jerylia stood and strapped her dagger to her thigh, allowing the light shift to fall over it, concealing the weapon.

"What part of 'there are Hrinthian soldiers in the streets looking for you specifically' do you not understand?" Faryn said as he placed a wet cloth on Gwera's forehead to cool her down.

"If I wear my headscarf they'll never know it's me, especially if I leave my sword here." She held her sword out to Adridia. "If there's even a scratch..." She didn't need to finish the warning before the warrior took the sword from her.

"I know. Don't worry." Adridia glanced up at the princess and the archer, her throat bobbing.

"Please be careful." The princess clapped her on the shoulder.

"Careful is my middle name."

"No," every other person in the room said before the sentence was even out of her mouth.

"You guys are mean." She wiped a non-existent tear from her eye. "We'll be back before you can say 'Faryn sucks'." She winked, ignoring Faryn's cries of indignation, and followed Theal out of the inn, her headscarf secure around her head, concealing most of her face. Business was starting to pick up at the Shrieking Cactus, patrons laughing loudly on the terrace.

"Excuse me." Jerylia flagged down the bartender, who immediately came over to them.

"How can I serve you?" he asked, glancing between them.

"I'm looking for Vael. I was told he frequents this establishment." The bartender leaned on the counter in front of him, a crooked smile on his lips. His eyes scanned her again, catching on her curves.

"Vael is a strange one. If you get bored with him, my shift ends in an hour." The princess grimaced and curled her top lip in disgust. She glanced at Theal who just shrugged, an amused smile playing at his mouth. The princess often received comments like this at certain taverns in Serradon and it never ended well for the person who said them.

She rolled her tongue around in her mouth, curling her finger at him to draw him forward. He leaned forward, gasping in surprise when she pinned him to the counter with a dagger through the neckline of his shirt. She leaned forward so her mouth was next to his ear. "You are a disgusting excuse of an elf and only a woman with no self-respect would sleep with someone like you." She pulled her dagger back, releasing him before turning to the rest of the bar. "This man has a small cock!" she announced before turning back to the bartender. "Now tell me where I can find Vael," she snarled. The bartender's face was now bright red as he pointed to the corner of the bar.

"Should have left well enough alone." Theal told the bartender before he followed Jerylia towards the back, hissing in her ear, "We were supposed to lay low." She only shrugged.

"He had it coming."

Vael was a well-groomed elf with long silver hair tied at the nape of his neck. His eyes glowed with age and he had an aura of wisdom around him. He spoke before the pair of companions could even sit down.

"You seek Caerin, the dragonslayer." He didn't even glance at them. "He resides in Greydell, a city long forgotten by the people of Hrinth." Jerylia swallowed, her throat suddenly dry. "I am sorry, but I do not hold the answers you seek. Visit Lilin at the Feather's Touch in Akah, to the north." Disappointment swelled in Jerylia's chest.

"Thank you, Vael." He nodded and they left the Shrieking Cactus.

"You're angry," Theal commented as they wove through the streets of Rert.

"I'm trying not to be. Caerin obviously doesn't want to be found. He was ostracized by his own people then locked away by another. I wouldn't want to be found if I were him either," Jerylia explained.

"Princess Jerylia!" Terror shot down her spine as a Hrinthian soldier stepped in front of her, flanked by six others. Eight more appeared behind them, surrounding them.

"Shit," she hissed.

"We can't take them. I can get back to the inn and get the others before they take you away." Theal stood in a protective stance, ready to give his life if necessary to protect his princess.

"No. I don't want them to know you and Faryn are shifters. Your blood is as valuable as gold." Shifter blood and saliva was a powerful ingredient to witches and were the main reason why shifters were rare. Most were killed or stolen away as infants to be harvested for their power.

"King Griel will be happy to see you." The soldier in charge pinned her wrists together behind her back and led them both to an armored carriage.

"King Griel?" Jerylia asked as they dragged her through the dusty street.

"The old king died two days ago. The eldest son was the heir to his throne," the soldier sneered as he threw them into the armored carriage. The lock clicked into place as they shut the door and soon the carriage was moving.

"Right, because this situation is so much better than the king knowing I'm a shifter," Theal quipped. The princess just gave him a sour look.

"They don't want you. They just want me." Jerylia was panicking trying to think of a way out.

"Jer, they're taking us to the capital. I can shift and fly out to get Faryn when they open the door to let us out." Jerylia chewed her lip as she weighed their options.

"Fine," she sighed in defeat. "But you and Faryn cannot come in arrows blazing to save me. It has to be a stealth mission. We can't risk any of us getting hurt."

"We will come for you. No matter what he does to you, remember that." Theal gripped her shoulder and pressed his forehead to hers. A tear slipped down her cheek.

"I have to tell you something. Just in case something happens to me," Jerylia sniffed, more tears falling from her eyes. "Adridia is going to kill me for telling you this but if I die, she'll shut down and you'll never know."

"What do you mean?" He pulled his head away from hers.

"You two have been burying your feelings for each other in other people. She feels the same about you as you do about her and she's been hiding it for my sake. I've known this for two years and I've felt guilty about it for two years." Theal was quiet for a moment before he folded the princess into his arms.

"You don't need to feel guilty about anything. Thank you for telling me, although I don't know what I'm going to do about it. She's a complicated woman with a one-track mind and right now her mind is on our mission, why we're here." Jerylia relaxed in his arms, comforted by the warmth of her friend.

"Do you remember when we and Faryn used to sneak out up to the witch tower?" Theal chuckled.

"Remember when the witches would give us a zap on the ass when they caught us messing with their potions?" Jerylia stifled a laugh.

"What happened after you drank that shimmery green potion? The one time we actually got you to drink something."

"I had webbed toes for a week," Theal admitted. He had

never told anyone that and had made sure to wear socks at all times during that week. Jerylia laughed loudly, the sound echoing off the metal walls around them. They settled back into silence.

"Have you mourned them yet?" he asked suddenly.

"Who?" she replied.

"Your father. Your prince. Your kingdom." He looked down at her. "You need to mourn. You've been shoving your feelings down deeper and deeper. It's not healthy." She pushed away from the comfort of his embrace.

"I don't have time to mourn. Especially not now. I'll mourn when we are safe and my mother is safe." He sighed, his heart clenching for his princess. She would hold her grief at bay for the sake of a kingdom that would probably never know her sacrifice. She folded her arms and turned away from him. The carriage rattled to a stop. "You have to go now." Jerylia wiped at her cheeks.

"Come back for me." Theal kissed her cheek before shifting in a flash of golden light. He let out a shriek as the soldiers opened the door, causing them to jump back.

"Stay strong, princess." He spoke into her mind, sending his love down that invisible thread between them as he shot into the night sky, the soldiers' shouts following him.

Chapter 18

Jerylia

She was thrown into a dark cell lined with sandstone bricks deep under the castle. The cell door shut with a bone-vibrating clang behind her. She sat up to get a bearing on her surroundings. The Hrinthian cell was nothing like the cells under the castle in Serramor. The cells in Serramor were constantly damp from the mountain snow-melt and the perfect environment for rats and mold. The cell she was currently locked in was dry, sand piled in the corners. There was a wooden bucket tipped over in the back corner opposite a wooden pallet topped with hay covered in a thin sheet. She brought her sandaled foot down on a black scorpion scuttling across bricks, her face twisting in disgust.

"It's unfortunate that you have to stay down here rather than in your room upstairs," Jerylia sighed, annoyance tugging at her bones. Griel's face appeared between the bars of her cell door.

"Your father was nothing but a puppet," she guessed as she collapsed onto the pallet in the corner.

"Clever princess," he smirked at her. "It's a shame you couldn't trust us enough to stay. All I wanted was to back the winning side of the war in Cordava. I knew you wouldn't be able to sit still. I knew you wouldn't be able to resist the lure of the dragonslayer. He probably doesn't even exist yet you gripped that thread of superstition tight." The now-king laughed at her. She ground her teeth together and folded her arms. "I have spies in place in Serradon, in nearly every city. Sinisstra received a message from me the moment you were discovered missing." Jerylia let out a dry laugh.

"You really had everything planned out, didn't you?" she mocked. He cocked his jaw, annoyed that she wasn't threatened by him.

"I guess you'll be happy to know your little companions will be safe. Sinisstra only requested you, in however many pieces it takes to extract the necessary information from you." He bared his teeth at her through the bars.

"I actually do have something to tell you. Hold on." She stood and crossed the cell to lean on the door, getting close to his ear. "Go fuck yourself," she whispered, pulling back with a grin. His hand flashed out, grabbing the front of her shift and slamming her against the bars. Pain flashed through her head as it smashed against the metal. She only smirked at him as he let go of her. "Worth it," she grinned. He grumbled and pulled back from the bars, stomping up the steps. The princess heaved a tired sigh and collapsed back on the pallet in the corner, her back to the door.

In the silence, her chest began to ache. She thought of her mother and father together, always smiling brightly. She pictured her father as he lay dying, using his last breaths to tell her mother how much he loved her. She remembered the last Asaydalas they celebrated together at Asaydil, the coastal city that hosted the summer palace. They had danced in the courtyard during the evening ball, pale columns rising around them. She had never felt safer than when he had twirled her around the colorful tile floor in his arms, her chiffon gown swirling around her ankles. Her father had insisted she dress nice for the occasion but hadn't told her why. His birthday was the day after the summer holiday and he had wanted to dance with his only daughter before he became officially old at six hundred years, almost three hundred years older than her mother.

"There's something I need to tell you on your twenty-sixth birthday," he had told her as he spun her around the courtyard. "Your mother and I decided it would be best if you knew."

"Why can't you tell me now?" she had asked, her curiosity piqued.

"You don't need to know until your powers manifest. My blood will... affect them," he had tried to explain without explaining.

"The dark elf blood?" she had asked. He had only nodded in reply and led her in the series of complicated steps that concluded the traditional dance.

Jerylia sat up in her cell, the gears spinning in her head. The conversation with her father that she had shoved to the back of her mind and the dreams with Serra had to be connected. They were both talking about something in her father's blood. She crossed her legs the way Gwera had taught her to center herself and tried to calm her mind. She closed her eyes and let her mind fall. A low humming began in the base of her skull. She thought of her connection to Serra and the life that grew from the earth. Flashes of green crossed her vision on the inside of her eyelids. Her eyes snapped open and she gasped loudly when fire exploded behind her eyes.

The cell had transformed before her. She was suddenly in her old room at the Hrithian royal palace, the sandstone bricks replaced by beautiful white marble and the shimmering tile mosaics. The princess blinked and the image was gone, replaced by the same dry cell. Maori leaned on the bars of the door.

"What was that?" Jerylia asked the dark elf. The princess

waved her fingers and the air around her rippled.

"I just needed to get your attention," she answered, turning her head to glance behind her. "I can't stay long. I wanted to offer you an explanation."

"Why don't we start with why your brother is a god-sized bag of elven assholes." Jerylia folded her arms across her chest and leaned against the wall. Maori chuckled quietly.

"Yes, that is true. I tried to talk him out of sending a message to Sinisstra. He won't listen to me. He didn't even listen to our father." Maori was silent for a moment. "I think he poisoned the old king," she whispered.

"He may be the king now but you are still royalty, don't you have a say?" Jerylia asked. Maori only scoffed at that.

"I'm royalty but I'm also female. We have an older sister. She was sold to the suitor with the highest dowry. She died giving birth because her body was so weak from the beatings, she couldn't handle it. Even Griel's wife fears for her life if the babe she bears is not a boy. Hrinth may seem like the perfect country from the outside but we treat our women like they are nothing."

"Sounds like Hrinth needs a change in leadership." Jerylia was sympathetic towards the women of Hrinth. She grew up privileged in Serradon, where women ruled and were treated as equals to men. She couldn't imagine growing up being told that she was meant to be nothing but a child bearer, that the greatest thing she could accomplish was bearing a talented son.

"I also wanted you to know that I appreciated having you as a friend during the short time we had you at the palace. I wanted you to know that it was real." Maori's eyes moistened with tears and Jerylia's heart softened. "You told me so many things about Serradon and taught me so much about the world. I've never been allowed to leave Hrinth so I know nothing except what I've read in books. You gave me something real that you can't get from words on a page and you gave me your friendship even when you had every reason not to trust me. I know you have your five companions that you would absolutely die for but I've never had anything close to that so it was real for me, our friendship was real."

"I never doubted that and our friendship *is* real." She offered the foreign princess a smile. Maori whipped her head around, her silken sheet of dark hair sliding over her shoulder.

"I have to go. I'll bring you extra rations, I promise." The princess waved goodbye, a mirage of soft sunlight filling Jerylia's cell for a few moments before it faded. Jerylia smiled to herself, warmth soothing the ache in her chest. She didn't feel sorry for the Hrinthian princess, she knew Maori wouldn't ever want that, but she felt sad that the women of Hrinth were treated like this. Why did males always insist they were better than the females of their own kind? Why couldn't they accept that every elf was created to be equal to one another? She laid down on her side, eventually giving in to the sleep that tugged at her eyelids.

She was woken abruptly by a hand grasping her arm and roughly pulling her upward. Her toes caught on the uneven stones, tripping her, but the hand never let go. She was dragged from the cell, feet sliding over the floor, trying to right herself. She grunted in pain as she felt her toenails bending backward and eventually ripping off as they went, her blood making the floor even more slippery. Up they went, her captor dragging her up three staircases and down a hallway before she was thrown before the foot of the Hrinthian throne. She quickly stood, refusing to lie prostrate before a foreign king, her feet screaming in pain. Griel smiled down at her wickedly, shadows flickering in the corners of the room. Her heart dropped into her stomach.

She knew that smile and she knew that more of her blood would be spilled before she was dragged out of this room.

"Not long ago you bowed before my father in this room. Will you not bow before me?" She levelled a bored look at him.

"I would rather shit in my hands and clap," she spat at him. He only chuckled darkly.

"Your mouth is going to get you in trouble, but since I am feeling generous tonight I will also allow it to be your saving grace." He glanced at the door to the left of the throne as Maori was escorted in by a guard, a hand on her lower back, uncomfortably low. Jerylia could tell by the tension in her spine that she didn't have a choice and that Griel could easily arrange for Maori what had happened to her elder sister. "Thank you for joining us, sister." The princess didn't look amused as she took up her place behind the throne. "You will enjoy this, I'm sure." He turned back to Jerylia. "Address me as the one true king of Hrinth and I promise not to further spill your blood. That's it. It's really quite simple."

"The true king of Hrinth is standing behind you." Griel glanced back, at Maori, before standing swiftly, rage taking over his features.

"You will address me as king!" His hand lashed out as he turned, striking Maori's cheek. She cried out, crumpling to the floor, but Jerylia knew better. The princess had the heart of a warrior. A mere slap would never make her crumble. Her heart ached as she wondered how many times Maori had quenched her fire to make the males in her life happy. How many times had she pretended to be a meek, obedient princess so no one would look twice at her? Her eyes met Maori's and her eyebrow raised in a single unspoken question. *Are you okay?* Maori nodded, almost imperceptibly as Griel turned back towards Jerylia once more, his robes swirling around him. He raised his arms, fingers forming claws, and the shadows lurking in the dark corners of the room lashed out, wrapping around her wrists and ankles, pulling her taut. They held her down, her back bowed and exposed. Solid footsteps vibrated the floor behind her and she craned her neck to see a large man in a hood striding towards her with a thick leather flog in his hand.

"I want to know everything you've learned about the dragonslayer and I want you to address me as King Griel when you tell me." Jerylia turned back towards the throne and snarled, letting every ounce of hate show in her eyes.

"Fuck. Off." Griel signaled with his hand. She braced herself for the pain. She heard a snap and then fire raked down her back, causing her to roar with pain. She'd experienced pain before but this was the worst pain she had ever felt. Every breath shifted the torn skin on her back, shooting fresh pain down her nerves. She took a couple of shaky breaths, steeling her nerves as she clenched her jaw. She was Jerylia 'Foebreaker' Serra, warrior princess of Serradon, next in line for the throne. She would not bow and she would not break, especially not for this entitled boy-king drunk on his own power. She forced every ounce of her rage and grief and power into her eyes as she met his, forcing herself to smile.

"This will only get worse. Tell me!" Only Jerylia had the talent to make a foreign king lose his composure. Her mother had always joked about it but here she was, making it a reality.

"Am I frustrating you, Griel? I've been told it's one of my best qualities," she ground out, letting her head droop forward.

"You will address me as king!" Jerylia lifted her head again, this time searching for Maori. The Hrinthian princess was standing again, a slight smile on her lips. Her eyebrow quirked up, this time asking the question. *Are you okay?* Jerylia closed her eyes slowly. *I will be.* Griel raised his hand. The flog snapped again. She strained against the shadows holding her as pain drew over her skin, biting back her screams. She would not give him the satisfaction of hearing them again. Strike after strike, she endured the torture. Her lip bled as her teeth pierced the skin. The muscles in her arms ached from straining against the shadows. After ten lashes, the shadows released her, and she fell to the floor, barely more than a bleeding sack of skin. Every movement, every jolt sent fresh pain down her back. All she knew was pain. She could barely think through it. Her eyes slid closed and she willed the goddesses to take her, to do anything to take away the pain.

"Take her back to her cell and send a healer down there with her. We'll do it again tomorrow." Griel stood and stalked out of the throne room.

The guards picked her up by her arms, their fingers brushing the torn skin of her back. A soft scream escaped her lips before a slap stung across her cheek. One of them told her to shut up before she felt them dragging her out of the throne room. The guards dumped her on the floor of her cell where she lay shaking in her own blood until a pair of healers laid their hands on her back. Instead of feeling pain at the contact, all she felt was relief. Warmth travelled down her spine and her skin began to itch as it knitted itself together. The fog of pain crept out of her mind.

"Please don't leave the scars," she whimpered. The healers glanced at each other.

"We have orders from the king to leave them." The princess closed her eyes as the healers finished their work. She didn't even have the energy to drag herself back to the bed in the corner after they left. So she lay on the crooked stones in the center of the cell and slept in a pool of her own drying blood.

Chapter 19

Faryn

"Faryn, I'm getting concerned." Adridia woke the dozing archer when she spoke as she paced the floor and checked the window again.

"About what?" he asked, stretching his arms above his head. His back ached from falling asleep in a small wooden chair next to the bed.

"Theal and Jer aren't back yet." Faryn glanced at the shadows growing longer over the floor.

"How long has it been?" he asked.

"A few hours. I'm going to go downstairs and see if they decided to stay in the taproom. Knowing Jer, they probably did." Adridia crossed the room in three strides, closing the door quietly behind her. Faryn leaned forward, resting his elbows on his knees.

"Oh." Gwera shifted on the bed, wincing as she brought her hand up to her head.

"You're awake." He scooted closer to the bed.

"With a pounding headache," she groaned and attempted to sit up.

"You kissed me," he commented. She huffed a laugh.

"Do *not* flatter yourself. I needed your saliva to stitch the wound shut without a scar." She leaned back against the headboard and reached for the water sitting on the bedside table.

"*My* saliva or shifter saliva?" he asked.

"You were carrying me and Theal wasn't." She shrugged and he nodded, smirking.

"Good. For a moment I thought you might have been sweet on me. It would have been devastating when I rejected you." She laughed, meeting his eyes. He knew, of course, where her interests lay. Gwera had been his closest friend and confidant since Jerylia had brought her into the squadron. They had spent many nights in her lavishly decorated rooms, drinking wine and discussing their innermost secrets. There was nothing he could hide from her nor she from him.

"You will find someone, Faryn. You deserve more than a princess who is meant for something more. She wasn't born for you," he scoffed.

"Thanks." He leaned back and folded his arms across his chest.

"Faryn, you are many things, but a ruler is not one of them. You were not made for Jerylia. Everything that has ever happened is controlled by the gods. They brought her parents together and made her for a purpose. You are not her purpose."

"This is not making me feel better, Gwere."

"I had a dream. I saw the triplet goddesses. I cannot tell you everything they revealed to me, but I can tell you this." She swung her legs over the edge of the bed so she could lean forward and grasp his hand. "Jerylia is meant for more than she knows and you cannot distract her from her path." He heaved a sigh. "And we both know that you do not truly love her. I believe you love her as a brother would. You were discontent with your life of bedding women so you turned your sights on the one woman you couldn't have, hoping she would fill that void in you, and then you blamed her when she saw through your intentions. You owe her an apology."

"I know. It feels like forever ago that I asked her to cancel her wedding the night before."

"One of your dumber moments." He scowled at the witch.

"I felt so foolish when she rejected me but I couldn't even blame her after all the years of boasting about the women I've bedded. So I lashed out, convinced myself it was her not me. Gods, I was so stupid." He shook his head and Gwera smiled softly at him.

"The clerk knew absolutely nothing. I have never met a more useless waste of space in my entire life!" Adridia stormed into the room, slamming the door behind her.

"What's going on?" Gwera asked as the warrior stalked to the window.

"Theal and Jerylia haven't returned yet. It's been hours."

"I can try to track them. Jerylia left her sword here and it's a powerful emotional tie." Gwera reached for the sword.

"You aren't going to do anything. You just woke up from a three-day nap." Faryn snatched the sword up before her fingers could even brush the hilt.

"So we're just supposed to sit here and wait for nothing to happen?" Gwera's eyes began to glow.

"Don't start that shit with me. It never ends well when you use your magic on me." The archer stood, towering over the petite witch.

"Guys, I think I see something." Adridia unlatched the window and opened the glass panes, leaning against the ledge. Something golden crashed into her, throwing both the warrior and the mysterious flying thing back into the room. Golden light flashed across the walls and there were suddenly two elves tangled in each other on the floor. Theal scrambled to his feet, launching towards the water Gwera had been sipping at. He emptied the contents of the glass and then the pitcher beside it, catching his breath.

"Theal, what's going on?" Faryn asked his twin.

"We were ambushed in the streets, probably because Jerylia made a scene at the tavern."

"Of course she did." Adridia rolled her eyes.

"They took us to the capital. I flew out of the carriage as soon as they opened it. We have to go get her." Theal met Faryn's gaze before looking at the other two elves in the room. "You two get to Akah. Look for Lilin at The Feather's Touch. We'll meet you there after we rescue Jerylia."

"No way we're splitting up. We all go to the capital together," Adridia countered.

"Faryn and I can get there by nightfall. It would take you and Gwera an entire day, maybe longer, to travel there and that's if we don't get lost as we did getting here. You two are going north. I'm not arguing about this. Jerylia is alone in a cell somewhere, maybe even being tortured." Theal crossed the room to the window. Faryn followed, preparing to shift.

"Fine. We'll meet you in Akah but we'll wait for you before we meet with Lilin." Adridia conceded. That was all Theal needed before he shifted and flew back out the window, Faryn directly behind him.

Shifting into an eagle was always a humbling experience. It started as tingling throughout his entire body and then the magic swept through him in a shock. Then he was flying, feeling the wind beneath and above his wings. His vision sharpened and he could see for miles around him. He propelled himself forward, trying to catch up with his brother. They soared over the shifting sands of the desert, racing against the sun dipping towards the horizon. They landed on a ledge outside a window-without-glass overlooking the grand throne room. Faryn lifted a wing and ducked his head, smoothing his feathers with his beak. Theal nudged him, flicking his head towards the window.

Jerylia's limbs were held by shadows, her back exposed to a tall man in a black hood behind her. His wrist moved and a flog ripped down her back. Faryn winced at the tension in her arms and the scream that died in her throat. He turned away from the scene for a moment as the anger filled his body. Jerylia would never want them to see her like this. The shadows slithered from her wrists, allowing her to slump to the floor. The prince stalked from the throne room and two of his guards dragged their princess towards the door, her bare feet sliding through her own blood. Rage shot through Faryn as he fluttered down to the gardens, shifting behind a thick cactus. He forced himself to take even breaths. Theal was beside him in a moment, drawing his bow. He brought a finger to his lips and pointed to the doorless archway that led into the palace. Servants emptied chamber pots into a sewer system that ran underground from a small port on the border of the garden. As soon as the servants disappeared, Theal placed a hand on Faryn's shoulder.

"You need to calm yourself, brother. Anger fogs the mind, makes for rash decisions. We need to be careful and stealthy about this." Faryn nodded, controlling the anger he felt in his chest.

"Let's go." They started for the door, sneaking silently along the shadows of the garden.

"You two are going to get hopelessly lost in there without help." Theal had his bow drawn back in an instant at the female voice that rang out behind them. Princess Maori stood with her hands folded behind her back, dressed in a gossamer nightgown that was open on the sides, showing most of her toned stomach.

"We're here for Jerylia and no one is going to stand in our way." Theal's voice held a death promise.

"I wouldn't dream of it." She walked past them to the palace archway, turning back to look at them as golden light lit up her features. "Come with me, please." The twins followed after her, wariness flooding their chests. They passed servants who didn't give them a second look. Faryn caught Theal's eye, raising an eyebrow.

"Don't make a sound," Maori whispered over her shoulder. Faryn was confused for a moment until her older brother strolled up to her, dressed in a long dark tunic.

"Did you promise the foreign princess extra rations, Maori?" His lips pressed together in a thin line.

"She needed it to heal after the flogging *you* put her through." The princess refused to cower in front of her brother, earning Faryn's respect immediately. Griel brought his hand up in a flash and there was a slapping sound. Maori clutched her cheek as he brought a hand up to grip her jaw.

"*I* am your king now and you are nothing. I will sell you to the highest bidder the first chance I get. Don't ever forget that," he hissed in her face before stalking off down the hallway. The princess took her hand away from her face and continued down the hall.

"How did he not see us?" Theal asked as soon as they had left the main palace and begun descending towards the dungeons.

"I can create mirages. I conjured an illusion that basically made you disappear. I could spend an hour explaining angles and light reflections to you but it would ruin the magic." She never stopped moving her feet as they kept going down the spiral staircase. "There's a guard at the bottom. Can you take care of that?" she whispered to them. Faryn nodded and unslung his bow from his back, nocking an arrow. He leaned over the railing, locating his target quickly. One breath in and out as he let the arrow fly. He hit the guard in the throat which was not a quick death but it was a quiet one. They descended the rest of the steps, stepping over the body at the bottom. The third door was Jerylia's cell and the archers both breathed a sigh of relief as they beheld her through the bars.

Her shirt lay in ribbons around her torso and her back, which was facing them, had been healed but still bore scars. They crisscrossed each other in a violently artful way. Blood was drying on the bricks beneath her as she slept deeply, her even breaths echoing off the sandstone around her.

"She looks broken." Maori tilted her head as they watched her sleep.

"After everything that's happened, our princess will never break," Faryn defended Jerylia, his voice low. "If she breaks, the world ends."

Chapter 20

Jerylia

Her dreams were memories. She was floating in nothing as she fell further into sleep. Then her eyes were open and she was a child again, growing into her large, pointed ears.

"Darling, I have someone I want you to meet." Her mother reached for her small hand, grasping it gently as she led her through the summer palace. The pale marble reflected the sun shining in from the huge, glassless windows. Jerylia lifted her face, listening to the waves crashing against the shore in harmony with the cries of the gulls.

"Who is it, Momma?" she asked eagerly, nearly running to keep up with her mother's long strides as they strolled through the halls of the summer palace. They entered the queen's chambers and a woman was standing there, waiting for them, in a thin white gown with a high neckline that cinched at the waist. Her dark hair was tied in a knot at the nape of her neck, the way most peasant women wore their hair.

"This is my new handmaiden," her mother explained as she released her daughter's hand. Jerylia stood straight, reaching up.

"It's nice to meet you." The handmaiden smiled as she shook Jerylia's small hand, performing a slight curtsy at the same time.

"The honor is mine, your highness," Jerylia giggled, not yet knowing the weight that title held.

"What happened to Madam Quilla?" she asked, looking up

at her mother with wide eyes.

"She retired to a little cottage in the mountains with her daughter," her mother explained. "But there are two more people I would like you to meet." The new handmaiden gestured to the bathroom doorway. Jerylia's curiosity piqued, she let go of her mother's leg and turned to see who might emerge.

"This is Faryn and Theal." Two heads of dark hair emerged from the bathroom. They both sported toothy grins as they approached.

"They are going to begin their training with you when we return to the capital," the queen told her.

"What are you training for?" Jerylia was required to be trained in all arts of death. Her mother would bring in combat masters from all over the continent but these two boys, who couldn't be more than three years older than her, could choose one specialty.

"Archery, all the way," one of the boys answered, pulling back the bowstring on an imaginary weapon.

"Archery for me too," the other boy replied, showing a little more decorum in front of the queen.

"I can't wait to learn swordplay. It's my mom's favorite too," Jerylia giggled, excited to have friends close to her age in the palace.

"Why don't you three go play in the courtyard?" The queen suggested and the three children raced off through the halls.

"Why are you starting your training so soon?" Theal asked her as they battled imaginary monsters in the courtyard.

"Every queen begins her training when she's eight. I will turn eight in a few months," she explained.

"I want to marry a queen," Faryn declared as he rolled across the tile. He puffed out his chest.

"You can't marry a queen, you're not a prince," Theal argued. Faryn stuck his tongue out at his twin.

"How old are you?" Jerylia asked. Amazed at how much taller than her the twins already were. Her forehead was square with Theal's chin.

"We just turned thirteen and mother decided we should begin training as warriors. She claims the idle life killed father too soon," Theal told her. Jerylia grew sad for her new friends. She couldn't imagine one of her parents dying.

"Let's go to the kitchens. The cooks always sneak me extra sweets." Faryn overheard them and shouted with joy as they raced into the palace.

Then she was eighteen with sweat dripping into her eyes as she sparred with a swordmaster from Draerige. His dark eyes glittered with disapproval as she let her shoulder drop, again.

"You are weak. Too weak to hold a sword properly." He snatched the sword from her hand. Anger flashed through her. Ten years of practice and she still couldn't wield a sword like her mother. "You will use weighted daggers and perform strength exercises every day. I can't go home until you are properly trained so you will do everything I tell you until I see my beloved country again." He stalked out of the training yard. Jerylia grit her teeth together as she smashed her fist into a straw training dummy.

"I could wield a greatsword when I was sixteen. He's right, you are weak." A tall blonde elf pushed herself off the wall she was leaning on, stalking towards the princess.

"And just who the fuck do you think you are?" the blonde smirked, sweeping into a dramatic bow.

"Adridia Ibyr." She stood up straight. At her full height, she would only be a few inches shorter than the Kaen twins. "I've been training as a swordswoman for ten years. I can wield a sword. What's your excuse?" She stepped closer to Jerylia.

"I've completed my training as a master assassin and a master of hand-to-hand combat in only ten years. That's my excuse."

"Jack of all trades, then, but a master of none."

"Oh good, you two have met." Both young women turned to see her mother stepping into the training yard, wearing practice armor, flanked by four other intimidating elves. "You've met my squadron many times. I trust this group of people with my life and we've seen many battles together. You are going to have your own squadron. Now that you're eighteen, I want you to start training together. Every single day so you can begin working together as a unit."

"Do I get to choose my companions?" she asked.

"I took the liberty of assuming you would choose the Kaen brothers and I chose another exemplary swordswoman."

"Who?"

"She's standing right next to you." Jerylia turned her head to look at the arrogant blonde next to her.

"I refuse. No." She folded her arms over her chest.

"I told you to choose your squadron a month ago and you failed to do so. You will work with Adridia Ibyr and you will not defy me." Her mother stood up straight. "If I find out you have stabbed her or harmed her in any way to get out of this, I will bear another daughter and name her my heir instead of you." Jerylia's face burned at the verbal lashing.

"Yes, my queen," she whispered, lowering her head.

"Good pup," Adridia sneered.

"And you. Just because I have defended you does not mean you can't be replaced. You are only five years older than her, you are little more than a child. I will not tolerate the ridicule of the crown. Jerylia is still your princess and future queen and you will treat her with the respect that title is owed." The blonde warrior flushed and nodded.

"Yes, your majesty." She caught Jerylia's eye before the princess retreated into the palace and what she saw there told her it would not be an easy battle to earn the warrior's respect.

That night, Jerylia was forced to stand at the head of the throne room with her mother as her three companions swore their oaths to her. As soon as the words left their mouths, three elves in black robes with ink etched into every inch of their visible skin entered the throne room. Jerylia watched as the tattooists inked a small wolf above the three warriors' hearts. Faryn caught her eye as the needle pierced his skin over and over and over, shooting her a lopsided grin.

Then Jerylia was barely older than twenty-two, riding through the dense mountain forests on horseback, a bow slung over her back. She had completed her sword training just four months ago and had immediately begun training with a bow. Her mother had not brought in a master and instead had enlisted Theal and Faryn to teach her instead.

"I'm freezing my ass off," she mumbled to herself as she uncorked her flask and took a deep drink of water. She could barely feel the tips of her fingers as she rubbed her hands together. A flash of green to her right drew her attention. "What the hell was that?" She squeezed her thighs, spurring her horse forward and eventually entered a clearing. A small cottage held attention at the center, smoke trickling from the chimney. The princess dismounted and approached the crooked front door.

"No, go away," a voice called from within before she could knock.

"I just need to warm up for a minute. Please," she answered back, hoping the door would swing open for her. The person inside heaved a sigh and the door indeed swung open but when Jerylia stepped inside, no one stood behind the door. A petite woman worked across the one-room cottage. The princess jumped as the door slammed shut behind her.

"Who are you?" The woman asked, turning to face her as she flicked her red hair over her shoulder.

"Um, Princess Jerylia, heir to the throne," she told the woman, shocked that the question had to be asked.

"My name's Gwera." The woman returned to her work after giving her a soft smile.

"What are you doing?"

"I've got many orders to fill, dear. It would be a waste of precious time to explain to you what they are." The woman finished sprinkling ingredients into a rounded glass bottle before setting it on the counter before her and holding her hands on either side of it. Her lips moved as she whispered and the bottle glowed green with magic. Jerylia's eyes widened.

"You're a witch!" she squealed with delight. "I've never met a witch before, well, one that didn't work for my mother." The woman sighed, corking the bottle before turning back to face the princess.

"Yes, I'm a witch. That's why I live out here and not in the city. I got tired of being blamed for every weird thing that happened. Now, is there something I can help you with because I've got to get these delivered before nightfall, or I won't be able to eat tomorrow." Jerylia grinned.

"Come with me and join my personal squadron." The witch blinked.

"I'm sorry, I must have heard you wrong."

"I want you to come with me to Serramor and join my personal squadron. My mother never had a witch on her squadron and I want to be different from her. You'll get to live in the castle and have a meal every day." Gwera looked skeptical. "I'll personally make sure the staff knows you are not to be blamed for anything weird." The witch laughed.

"I need a week." Tears were welling in her eyes. "I need a week to get everything settled here and then I'll be at the castle." She sniffed, the tears falling over her cheeks. "Serra answered my prayers with you, her descendant. I promise I will do anything you need me to do." She smiled and shook Jerylia's hand.

The princess woke, startled by keys rattling against the metal lock on her door. She sat up, her clothes falling in shreds around her. Princess Maori swung open the door to her cell and tossed her a clean white shift.

"What are you doing?" Jerylia asked, confusion clouding her mind.

"Helping a friend." She smiled and turned to her right. Jerylia could have wept at the relief that swept through her when the Kaen twins emerged from the shadows. She stood on shaking legs and stumbled to the door, wrapping the brothers in a tight embrace.

"Come with us," she whispered to the princess, reaching out to squeeze her hand.

"I can't. Someone has to keep an eye on Griel." Jerylia pulled back.

"If it gets to the breaking point, come find us in Greydell. We're on the trail of the dragonslayer. Find Lilin at the Feather's Touch in Akah." Maori nodded as Jerylia turned to her friends, pulling the shift over her torn shirt. As soon as the shift was in place, she pulled the shirt off from under the shift, leaving it in tatters on the floor.

"Get me the fuck out of here."

Chapter 21

Jerylia

The ishtuk beneath her was not well-groomed and stunk of bird shit as it raced across the desert. The twins flew above her, swooping down to brush a wing past her leg every few minutes. She was exhausted and her back itched from the quick healing that was done. The twins had told her it would take a few days to get to Akah where Gwera and Adridia were waiting for them, even at the swift speed she was moving on the oversized bird.

"*Do you need one of us to ride with you so you can sleep?*" Theal flew close to her as he spoke over the invisible cord that stretched between them. She couldn't do much more than nod, her use of magic without practice as well as the deep tissue healing she was still doing, using up every last bit of her energy. There was a golden flash and then Theal sat behind her on the large bird, which gave a high-pitched trill at the sudden extra weight. She leaned back against him and her eyelids slid shut.

"*Not this shit again,*" *she grumbled as she opened her eyes to the mist-filled forest once again.*

"*You're neglecting your heritage.*" *Serra appeared before her.*

"Then tell me what you want me to do. No riddles. No cryptic messages. Just please tell me."

"*I'm afraid I can't do that.*" *The goddess turned to face her and Jerylia gasped. She looked different. That golden glow was* diminished, wrinkles appearing around her eyes. A thin silver streak of hair disappeared underneath the golden crown wrapped with ivy on her head. "Do you know what I am, what all the gods and goddesses are?"

"We are taught that you're Fae, the most powerful among your kind."

"My sisters and I are the only surviving Fae from Serradon. The rest are long dead, their bloodlines carried on in our children, the elves. Our reign is coming to an end because, after thousands of years, the bloodlines have crossed and the Fae are emerging from history once again." Serra's features became serene and her mouth tilted up in a satisfied smile.

"I hope you're not speaking of me. I don't want that responsibility."

"You don't have a choice." All the peace was gone in an instant and the goddess was snarling at the princess. "You are my champion. And you must defeat Jash's champion before she tears apart the fabric of death."

"The Draerigian god of death?" Jerylia's mind was swimming, the cords crossing and tangling as she tried to unravel the complicated knot.

"You must find Della's champion. He lives in blissful ignorance of the war that is coming and it will be his undoing." Serra grabbed her shoulders.

"What about Vay? Shouldn't the god of life's champion be the one to bring down the god of death's?" Serra's eyes widened and her grip relaxed as her gaze lifted.

"Vay." She smiled, her features so soft all of a sudden as her eyes grew distanced. "He and Jash are twins, you know, or they were. Jash killed him when you were born." Her eyes met Jerylia's and overwhelming sorrow filled the air between them.

"Jash had hated him ever since he and I became lovers. And then when you were born..." She trailed off.

A shadow appeared behind her, flames dancing where the eyes should be.

"Wake up," Serra hissed.

The princess jerked awake, her fingers gripping the leather reins on the ishtuk tight.

Theal's grip on her waist tightened as she threatened to topple.

"How long was I asleep?" she asked, blinking at the sun in her eyes. Her skin had grown red and heat radiated off of her.

"A while. The sun should be going down within the hour." His hands moved away from her waist now that she was stable on the large bird. "Do you want to make camp for the night?"

"No. The sooner we get to Akah the better." Serra's words echoed in her mind. Where the hell was she supposed to find another reborn fae in a world full of pointed ears?

"You were mumbling in your sleep," Theal commented.

"Serra visited me again. She never offers any answers, just more questions." The princess rolled her shoulders back and sighed. Theal was quiet behind her.

"I'll leave you alone to think." The sun was suddenly warm on her back as golden light flashed from behind her. Two birds were soaring above her again.

The night seemed longer than the day and the dunes around her seemed as endless as her thoughts. She felt as if the answer was just beyond her grasp, the tips of her fingers just brushing against it. She ran her tongue over her teeth. Didn't the fae have elongated canines? Her teeth were nothing but ordinary. So many thoughts rattled around in her mind as she rode through the night and most of the next day. The afternoon sun bathed the sandstone buildings of Akah in a golden light. The princess yawned as she steered her ishtuk down the dusty streets.

"Jerylia!" Her heart stuttered when she heard someone call her name. Gwera's red hair stood out, stark against the black hair of the dark elves. She slumped in relief and a smile stretched over her mouth.

"You smell like shit." Adridia clapped her on the shoulder once she reached them, pulling them both into a tight embrace.

"We missed you." Gwera refused to let go of her, the witch's short arms nearly crushing her ribs.

"Don't ever get kidnapped again. We were worried sick." She pulled away and gripped Jerylia's chin, examining her face, searching for any sign of injury. She felt tendrils of magic slither up her back and recoiled.

"I'll try not to." Jerylia smiled, genuinely, for the first time in weeks.

"We need to discuss how we are going to make the new King's death long and painful," Faryn said to Adridia.

Chapter 22

Adridia

Even without the other three members of their squadron, the warrior and the witch were slow-moving across the desert.

"I swear to Serra if they put one hand on her I will rip someone's spine from their body." Adridia was fuming as they rode across the desert on camels, having been unable to afford ishtuks.

"I have been listening to your threats for the past four hours and they have not gotten more creative. Frankly, I'm disappointed," Gwera said in a monotone.

"Don't you have a magic thing that you can use to at least let us know that she is okay?"

"That is not how my magic works and you know that."

"Do you at least know how long it will be until we reach Akah?"

"Just another hour or two. Then we have to occupy ourselves until the twins get here with Jerylia." Gwera rolled her shoulders back.

"How's your leg?"

"Just a bit achy. I should be perfect by tomorrow."

"Oh, Gwera, you're always perfect," Adridia mocked in a high-pitched voice.

"You're joking, but you're right," Gwera chuckled.

"I've been thinking…" Adridia began after a long silence.

"Oh, Serra, help us," Gwera grumbled. The warrior just glared at her.

"How do you suppose our dear princess is planning on convincing this dragonslayer to help us?"

"With her charm, probably."

"Oh, we are so fucked." Gwera grinned at Adridia.

"I'm sure she's planning on bribing him, but I have been musing over a backup plan."

"That's a good idea. What can you use to bribe a man who lives in absolute paradise, alone with his dragons?"

"You know, I've been thinking about his name, tossing it around in my head." Gwera lifted a hand to allow a cool breeze to flow over them. "My grandmother's maiden name was Ocealith. My mother used to speak of a disgraced cousin who disappeared long before I was born."

"So there's a possibility that this dragonslayer is your cousin?" Gwera nodded. "Small world," she mused as their camels lumbered into the desert city. The two women dismounted and left the animals with the local camel caretaker.

"I've been itching for a new tattoo," Adridia commented as they strolled through the street markets. She eyed a row of bottles filled with dark ink.

"Me too," Gwera agreed, following the warrior's eye line. Her shift fluttered in the warm breeze as she sauntered up to the stall, handing the vendor a gold coin before scooping up a jar and set of needles. They continued down the street until they came across an inn. The keepers of the inn fussed over them, chattering on and on in Hrinthian. Gwera's eyes glowed a gentle green for a moment as she listened to them.

"They don't get many guests out here and would like to offer us their biggest room at a small discount," she explained.

"I can't believe I'm about to say it, but I miss Jerylia's royal studies." It was easy for them to forget the well of information their princess held thanks to her endless rotation of tutors but she was always quick to remind them.

The innkeepers led them up the steps into the upper levels of the sandstone building. She gestured to a worn wooden door with a cactus-shaped plaque in the center of it. The woman quickly thanked them and disappeared back down the stairs. The room was filled with natural light thanks to the glassless windows that stretched across two of the four walls. A pile of cushions served as a sofa and there were three colorful beds consisting of a large base cushion big enough to comfortably fit a tall elf, maybe two, and a multitude of pillows on top. Incense lanterns were hung from chains around the room, the smoke filling the room with a spicy smelling haze. It was a beautiful room which made Adridia wonder why the inn was struggling with business, especially if all the rooms looked like this one.

"I'll sleep on the cushions since I'm the smallest." Gwera tossed her bottomless satchel onto the cushions and flopped down beside it, moaning as she sank deeper into the pillows. "Remind me to sell my bed and get one of these when we get back home."

"Shall we also take the glass out of the windows?" Adridia joked. Gwera shivered as she remembered the cold, mountain winds. The castle was constantly warm due to the numerous torches lining the halls and the huge hearths in every room, but anywhere outside, especially during the winter season, the sharp wind could cut through clothing as easily as a knife. Gwera quickly composed herself and scooted to the edge of her cushion pile to arrange the ink jars on the floor.

"What were you thinking?" Adridia sat on the floor cross-legged and jerked her chin towards the jars.

"First I was thinking of doing the Hrinthian symbol for a dragon but now I'm thinking about this." She held her hands up and a symbol glowed above them.

"That's the symbol the servants of the Fae wore on the backs of their necks. It's why we still tattoo our roles on the back of our necks. What does that have to do with us?" She still remembered the day they inked the small sword on the back of her neck. It had been her second tattoo, the first being the sleeve of ocean waves that covered her entire arm. She had never felt pride like she did when they put that symbol there, the symbol she had chosen along with the role of swordswoman. Adridia gaped at the glowing symbol, questions filling her mind.

"While I was unconscious, healing myself, the triplet goddesses paid me a visit. They told me something." She lowered her hands and the symbol dissipated. "We were taught that the gods and goddesses we serve are Fae, the most powerful among their kind."

"Every elfling knows this," Adridia snorted, stretching her legs out in front of her.

"The gods have chosen their champions," she whispered. "Jash chose Sinisstra and manipulated her. He's still angry over what happened with Vay."

"What happened to Vay?" Adridia was clueless about the lives of the gods.

"Serra and Vay were mates for millennia. Jash hated the northern Fae and despised their bond. When Jerylia was born, Jash killed Vay." Gwera explained as she picked out a needle and gestured for Adridia to lay down.

"Why then?" She complied with Gwera's request and pulled her shift up to reveal the bone of her hip. She grit her teeth as

Gwera lifted the needle using her magic and began to etch the symbol into her skin.

"He was weakened. He gave up his power to his champion."

"Who is his champion?" The warrior's heart was thundering in her chest.

"Jerylia is special. Vay bestowed his power upon her through his descendant, the Blacksmith of the North."

"Her father, he's part dark elf." Adridia winced as the needle pierced a particularly sore spot.

"And Serra also bestowed her powers, although hers were expected." Adridia made a choking noise.

"She has the power of two gods inside of her?" Gwera nodded.

"There's more to it."

"How could there be more?" She barely even noticed the needle anymore as she tried to process the new information.

"Jerylia is Fae."

"But she looks like an elf."

"She has to burn away her elven body before she can truly wield her powers."

"Does Della have a champion?" Gwera grinned.

"Caerin Ocealith."

"He's not even Hrinthian." Adridia made a sour face.

"He lives in her realm and that story Peld told about the deal between the gods, it was true. Asayda's champion is Hrinthian. The gods have laid their plans to destroy Jash."

"So, who is Asayda's champion? And Eowessa's?" Gwera's forehead creased with concentration.

"Their champions have been chosen but not made known to me."

"But we have to find them, right? They'll be powerful

enough to turn the tide against Sinisstra."

"Sinisstra is not alone anymore. The god of Fastille, Jonik, and the androgynous deity of Saeroc, Eldrin, have chosen their champions who have sided with Sinisstra."

"Fuckers," Adridia muttered.

"Torith's goddess, Fayeth, has yet to make her champion known but I feel they will easily be swayed to our side because of Kaed."

"Do the other two countries not know that Sinisstra slew their princes in cold blood as a show of power?"

"I'm afraid that they do and are following her out of fear, but Torith has never bowed so easily."

"So Jerylia will be a Fae. With all the Fae things." Adridia's mind was blown.

"She'll have an animal form and a mating bond but that's about the extent of it. She could form a court if she felt like it, but considering she'll be a queen someday as well as a living goddess, I doubt she will." Shifter elves, like Theal and Faryn, retained the Fae ability to shift into an animal form but they were rare. Mating bonds were much more common but chosen, unlike Fae bonds. During sex, if both elves choose to activate a bond, the mating bond snaps into place. Its effects are not as potent as a Fae bond but still intoxicating. As the Fae courts grew in size, they turned into kingdoms, ruled by the direct descendants of the most powerful Fae beings.

"Sounds like she'll be able to handle this war all by herself."

"Jash has taken over Sinisstra's soul. He manipulated her into using forbidden magic. He got her to open a doorway into the realm of the gods. They retired to another realm to govern this one without the ability to interfere. It wasn't until they saw that we needed Fae to roam our lands once again, to help hold the peace, that they were allowed to interfere." Gwera lowered her hands and the needle fell to the wooden floor. Adridia propped herself up on her elbows to admire the dark ink contrasted against her pale skin.

"I like it." Her skin was red and blood welled around the dark lines but there was a satisfaction in the stinging pain radiating through her hip.

"Servant of the Fae," she said with a grin. It was a badge she would forever wear with pride.

Chapter 23

Jerylia

Gwera and Adridia led them through the streets back to the inn. The innkeepers greet them with broad smiles and enthusiastic voices. She smiled and thanked them in Hrithian, to which they responded by shaking her hand and gesturing up the stairs. She smiled and said her goodbyes before following her companions up the stairs to the room they had rented.

"Having fun, were we?" She raised an eyebrow at the ink and blood smeared on the floor. Adridia grinned and lifted her shift to reveal a fresh tattoo on her hip. Theal coughed and shuffled away as Gwera lifted her own shift to reveal a matching symbol. Jerylia rolled her eyes at the quiet shifter. Honestly, it was as if he'd never seen a woman naked.

"Servant of the Fae?" Faryn tilted his head in question. Jerylia gasped.

"Is that what she meant?" All the vague answers clicked together, like puzzle pieces.

The picture was still incomplete but at least now she could begin to make sense of things.

"Serra enjoys being cryptic. When she visited me, her sisters were there to explain everything."

"Well, then can you tell me because as soon as she started talking about Vay, her grief took over." Gwera nodded and sat down on the floor, picking up a silver tattoo needle.

"Boys lay down." Theal and Faryn shared a look that only twins could before laying on the floor, one on each side of Gwera. She flexed her fingers and the needles floated through the air, the green magic causing them to glow. She tattooed the same symbol into their hips as she explained everything to them. Jerylia sank further into the mountain of cushions as her mind spun with confusion.

"I think you broke her." Adridia poked her cheek and she snapped her head to the side, teeth clicking together very close to Adridia's extended finger.

"Careful, I bite." She grinned as the warrior pulled her hand back all too quickly.

"Please don't get blood on my bed," Gwera deadpanned as she wiped the excess blood and ink from the floor.

"Have you had time to find The Feather's Touch?" Jerylia asked as she stood and began fastening her dagger strap around a muscled thigh.

"It's not far down the street. The brothel is the reason the inn's business has dwindled," Gwera commented as she placed a pile of copper coins on the floor in front of her. She held her hands over the money and began whispering in the ancient tongue. A few moments later the coins glowed green and when the glow faded, gold had taken their place. She stood after scooping up the pile of coins. Jerylia raised an eyebrow when she marched directly over to her and placed her hands on her cheeks, whispering a few words.

"What are you—" Gwera shushed her before continuing. The princess felt a tingling in her face and scalp before the witch finally pulled away.

"While we are going in and out of the cities, you will wear a different face. I've been working on a more permanent glamour, almost like changing your skin except your true skin will always be underneath. I can remove the glamour once we head into the mountains." Jerylia scrambled to find the nearest mirror. She squeaked as she took in her reflection. Gwera had made her into a dark elf. Her skin was a steel grey and her hair had turned into the deep silky shade of black all dark elves sported. Black freckles dotted her cheeks and arms and her lips had grown fuller. Her entire face was different, longer with sharper cheekbones and round brown eyes.

"I'm beautiful." She touched her face and ran a hand down the length of her silky smooth hair that fell to her hips.

"This is what you would have looked like had your father been a fully dark elf, even with your mother's line. All I had to do was bring forward the darker genes," Gwera explained as she rinsed her hands in the washbasin. "We really should be going. We've wasted enough time as it is and the twin moons will rise soon." She gathered her bottomless satchel and hauled it over one shoulder.

They headed out the door, the twins opting to stay back. The streets were becoming more boisterous as night fell, the drunks feeling bolder in the dark. Jerylia dodged a pot-bellied elder as he stumbled towards her, his black skin making him near invisible. She made a face at the smell radiating off of him and continued until they reached a large tent with lanterns decorating the outside. She ran her fingers over the warm glass of one, fascinated by the red flame. They pushed their way through the thick flaps and were immediately assaulted by heavy smoke. Jerylia coughed as her eyes watered. Shadows danced around the tent in odd ways, stretched by the thick smoke.

"It's the drug made from snow flowers," Gwera said as her hand fluttered in front of her face, trying to clear the smoke from her nose. But more rose to take its place and soon they were all feeling the effects.

"We need to find Lilin," Jerylia said, her voice sounding very far away. Her skin tingled and her brain felt like it was floating in her skull. She smiled to herself as a strange calm overtook her and she began to giggle.

"Oh, Serra," Adrida grumbled. The larger elf seemed to not feel anything at all. "I forgot, you've never experimented with anything but alcohol." The warrior clamped a heavy hand on her shoulder and led her through the tent to the main chamber. Jerylia's eyes widened when she saw all the elves, male and female, dancing for different patrons.

"They're naked," she hissed to Adridia before breaking into a fit of giggles again.

"They're lucky." Gwera pulled at her shift absentmindedly. "I'll bet the smoke feels so good on the skin." She lifted the hem, revealing her legs little by little.

"Yes, be free," Jerylia cheered for her friend.

"Stop that." Adridia fixed Gwera's shift for her. "You don't want to be naked here, they'll think you'll dance for them," Gwera gasped loudly.

"I would love to dance for them." She stretched her arms above her head and twirled once before Adridia caught her again.

"Let's just find Lilin and go back to the inn. You can dance there." Gwera nodded with a relaxed smile on her lips. Her eyes were hooded, almost closed.

"Why aren't you feeling anything?" Jerylia frowned and poked Adridia's cheek. The warrior sighed.

"I am, I just have more control than you two apparently do. There's a drug similar to this in Serradon, except you don't smoke it. You crush it into a powder and pull it into your nose through a small paper tube. I've built a resistance so I can still retain my dignity in this." She waved a hand around them, disturbing the smoke. She took a deep breath and cringed. "Although this stuff is extremely strong." She pulled them forward to sit on a set of matching cushions. A thin woman wearing a thin white shawl and a sheer veil over her mouth and nose approached them.

"Welcome to the Feather's Touch." Her voice was mesmerizing and Jerylia found herself lingering on every syllable that left her lips. "Who would you like?" She glanced down at the wooden board in her hand, a long quill poised above it.

"Lilin, please," Adridia told her. The woman bit her lip and scanned the board.

"Fifty coppers, twenty-five silvers, or ten gold pieces." Gwera fished in her satchel for a moment before drawing out a handful of coins.

"Is this enough?" she whispered loudly to Adridia as she handed her the coins. The woman in white raised an eyebrow at her inebriation but said nothing. Adri sighed and handed the coins to the woman who slid them into a small leather pouch slung around her narrow hips.

"Lilin will be with you momentarily." She lowered her board and disappeared into a room separated by more tent flaps and a shiny gold rope.

"Have you done this before?" Jerylia asked her friend as she ran her hand over the large cushion underneath her. It was so soft.

"I like to visit the brothels in Serradon. The workers aren't used to being treated well and I like to give them a night off from the abuse." Jerylia smiled and leaned over, resting her head on her friend's shoulder.

"You're a good person," she mumbled. Her body felt so

heavy and her muscles were beginning to twitch. She sat up when a dark elf emerged from the side room, heading straight for them. She was naked like the others and her body was thin with very little muscle, yet she was curvy with generous assets on both her chest and behind. Her skin was a deep grey, much darker than Jerylia's glamoured skin and her hair was pulled up high on her head, held with a shiny gold ring embedded with jewels.

"Good evening." Her voice was light and airy as if she enjoyed doing this. Her sharp eyes caught on Adridia. "I assume you are the one I am dancing for."

"Actually, we're here for some information." Adridia pulled Gwera back down when she tried to get up to touch Lilin's hair.

"I love your hair," the witch mumbled as she stared with wide eyes.

"Thank you, I was born with it." She turned back to Adri. "What information?" she asked as she began to dance, her arms lifting above her head as her wrists rolled over and over. Jerylia was unable to tear her eyes away from the beauty in front of her.

"You don't have to do that," Adridia told her. Jerylia shook her head, never wishing for Lilin to stop.

"Yes, I do. It is what you paid for." Her feet moved quickly underneath her as she began to move all parts of her body.

"We're looking for the dragonslayer, Caerin Ocealith." Lilin cracked a smile as she danced.

"I've been waiting for the day when someone would ask after him. I cannot tell you how to reach Greydell, but I can send you towards someone who can." She span again. "Speak to Sessa in the market of Sek. She will point you in the right direction." Disappointment swelled in Jerylia's chest.

"Thank you." Adridia smiled warmly at the dancer. "I'm going to get these two back to the inn before they crash." Lilin smiled back at her like they were sharing a joke.

"Hey, you can't talk about us when we're right here." She protested. Adridia just rolled her eyes and hauled them to their feet.

"Where are we going? Oh, the room is spinning." Gwera swayed on her feet. "Carry me, brave warrior." She draped herself onto Adridia who just shoved her off. "I can barely carry myself." Jerylia gave a small wave to Lilin as they left, who just smiled at her.

The streets were different when they left the tent. The air was no longer thick in her lungs and it was as if she could hear the stars flickering high above them. She closed her eyes and turned her head up towards the sky, allowing Adridia to pull her along. She felt herself falling, drowning in all the sounds of the desert city. They swallowed her whole, washing over her in a tidal wave of sensory overload. Everything was just a little bit louder and she could feel her mind snagging on certain things, replaying them in her mind over and over again for no reason at all. She almost wished she could feel like this forever, lost in her own mind with no responsibility or threat looming over her.

"What the hell did you do to them?" Faryn asked as they stumbled into their rented room at the inn, Jerylia and Gwera collapsing in a fit of giggles on the pile of cushions.

"Turns out they fill the brothel with smoke from that snow flower drug. It's quite potent." She frowned at the two women currently laughing to each other.

"I can tell," Theal commented. He was trying to hide a smile. "What did Lilin tell you?"

"We have to find *another* mysterious person in the next town north of here to find the dragonslayer, blah, blah, blah." Jerylia played with the silky ends of her hair as she spoke.

"Well, at least you got to try drugs while we were here," Adridia commented, dragging a hand through her short hair.

"Now I wish I'd gone with you. It's been a while since I've been *that* high," Faryn said as he pulled his shirt off and climbed into one of the beds.

"So who do we have to find?" Theal went over to the washbasin and scooped some water before running his hands over his hair.

"Sessa in Sek." Gwera was asleep before she finished speaking. Jerylia giggled, repeating the words over and over again out loud, laughing each time.

"Serra's tits!" Faryn grumbled from his bed. "Not another fucking desert trek."

Chapter 24

Jerylia

Sek was an absolute shithole. Instead of ishtuks, camels were the favored mode of travel, which means instead of the thin white liquid that usually comes out of ishtuks and soaks into the sand, big steaming piles of camel shit littered the streets. Every day the mountains grew closer and Jerylia grew a little more homesick. She found her thoughts drifting to the mountain peaks of her home and lost herself in her most treasured memories of her father. She had an ache in her chest that wasn't going away and she felt off, though she couldn't quite place why. Something loomed inside of her, preparing to attack anything that provoked it.

The market was busiest around the middle of the day. It took them three days just to find Sessa's stall. Three days too long in this stinking cesspool of a town. With each passing day, Jerylia's irritation grew. She felt herself teetering on an edge and anything could push her over into the sea of anger waiting below, bubbling just beneath the surface. On the third day of looking, they approached an old lump of a woman squatting behind a jewelry stall.

"I'm looking for Sessa, do you know where I can find her?" Gwera asked, flashing a brilliant smile. The woman just curled her upper lip at the witch.

"Who's asking?" Her voice was rough as she spoke.

"A friend," Gwera offered. The woman just stared at her, obviously unamused. Jerylia rolled her eyes at her. She untied the coin pouch from her belt and shook it, rattling the gold pieces inside.

"Customers." The princess pushed forward to lean against one of the wooden support posts on the stall.

"I'm Sessa. What do you want?" She pushed forward two velvet-covered trays, each covered with meticulously organized jewelry.

"Information. We each buy something from you and you tell us where we can find Caerin Ocealith." Jerylia tossed the leather pouch between her hands. Sessa stared at her for a moment, contemplating what she was offering.

"You each have to get something or no deal." She narrowed her eyes at all of them. Jerylia quickly chose two small silver rings to pierce her nose with. Theal and Faryn grabbed matching leather cords to go around their wrists and Gwera picked up a simple beaded bracelet, mumbling something about enchanting it. Adridia chose a tiny gold hoop, holding it up to her eyebrow and winking. Jerylia plopped a small stack of gold pieces on the wooden counter.

"Now talk." Sessa swiped the gold off the counter, sifting through the coins as she spoke.

"Talk to the blacksmith, Teak. He works in Setent."

"Setent is all the way over on the coast," Jerylia sputtered. Sessa just shrugged.

"Sounds like your problem," she sneered as she turned.

"Asshole." Jerylia attempted to leap over the stall counter but was pulled back by each of her arms, one held by Adridia, one held by Theal.

"Why don't we go find something to drink?" Faryn

suggested, taking off in the direction of the tavern they had been staying at.

A few mugs of ale later, Jerylia's anger had been smothered and replaced by the warm feeling of alcohol in her blood. Faryn was currently losing an arm-wrestling competition against Adridia. Jerylia leaned back in the booth and smiled as she took another drink of her beverage.

"That's not fair, I've had more to drink than you have," Faryn muttered, sulking in his seat.

"Or I'm just better than you," she smirked, drinking deep from her cup. Theal only smiled as he glanced towards the warrior quickly. Jerylia rolled her eyes. Their unwillingness to talk to each other about their feelings was beginning to grate on her nerves. Her anger had dissipated for the moment but she knew it wouldn't take much for her to snap again.

"Why don't we play a round of drink or dare?" She leaned forward.

"Now things are getting interesting." Gwera cocked an eyebrow.

"Faryn, stand up and dance like an ishtuk," Adridia started. Faryn rolled his eyes but complied, dancing around the bar like a flightless bird, arms tucked into his side in an odd way that made his elbows stick out to the side while his legs bent at the knee and his head bobbed back and forth. While Adridia and Theal were distracted, Jerylia leaned over to whisper to Gwera.

"We're both having the same idea, right?" Gwera nodded, her eyes flicking back and forth between Theal and Adri. Jerylia nodded, leaning back in her seat as Faryn finished his dance and rejoined them.

"All right, Gwera." He levelled his eyes at the witch. "Cut your hair." He laid his hand flat and levelled it at his shoulder, indicating length. She narrowed her eyes at him and snapped her fingers. Her hair instantly shortened itself to a blunt cut, ending just below her shoulder, the curls straightening themselves out. Faryn just shook his head. "No, cut it. Not just a glamour." Gwera just swirled her wine around in the glass in front of her.

"This is what my hair actually looks like. I use the same permanent glamour I used on Jerylia. The long hair makes me look more approachable and this cut is a common witch style." Jerylia's eyes widened. "If I keep it short like this, it's easier to change."

"Not what I was expecting." Even Theal, the unshockable, was shocked.

"Jerylia, why don't you try to use your power?" Gwera dared the princess. She froze. The power was there, lying just under her skin. All she had to do was reach for it, but without a leash, a form of control, there was no telling what she would do in the crowded tavern. So instead, she tilted her cup up to her lips and finished her drink.

"That scared?" Faryn teased. Jerylia just glared at the table in front of her, her good mood suddenly soured.

"Yeah, Jer, grow a pair. Let's see those awe-inspiring powers." Adridia was grinning.

Anger flared through the princess. It wasn't their fault, they just didn't understand. They didn't have the weight of everything on their shoulders. They couldn't accidentally level the town with a simple, uncontrolled thought. They weren't chosen by the gods to bring peace to the planet, which is absolute bullshit. She didn't get to choose. She just had the weight of the world dropped on her shoulders without even an explanation. She breathed deeply through her nose, trying to calm herself but her thoughts kept spiraling out of control, fueling the anger burning through her.

"Just leave it alone, please," she mumbled, her eyes searching for the serving maid to order another drink.

"Just try, Jer." Gwera laid a small hand on her arm in a failed attempt to be comforting.

"I said leave it alone!" She stood suddenly, the wooden bench behind her shifting from the movement, and her companions just stared at her, as if she'd grown another head. She ran a hand through her hair, combing it out of her face in an attempt to hide the way her fingers were shaking.

"What the fuck, Jer?" Adri asked. Jerylia scoffed and scooted out of the booth, clenching one of her hands into a fist, focusing on the pain of her fingernails piercing the skin instead of the rage swirling under her skin. She attempted to head towards the stairs towards the rear of the building that led to the rooms upstairs but was stopped with a hand around her wrist. "Jerylia, what is wrong with you?" Adridia was the one holding her wrist, her eyes full of sympathy, and that somehow made it all worse. She'd been doing so well at holding it all together but had neglected to actually face her grief and now it was going to consume her. The rage in her chest crawled up and exploded out of her mouth, the words biting.

"What's wrong with me? How about what's wrong with you? Why are you all trying to act like we have any hope of defeating Sinisstra? Why are we acting like our home isn't in the grip of enemy hands? Why are we acting like my father isn't dead and my mother isn't most likely stuck in a dungeon enduring who knows what kinds of torture?"

"We can't control any of that, so it doesn't do well to worry about it until we can." Theal had come up to stand next to Adridia. They were the wrong words and it wasn't his fault but she didn't have another target so she did what she did best and aimed for the heart, focusing on doing as much damage as possible. Jerylia ripped her arm out of the warrior's grip, a dry laugh bubbling from her lips.

"Oh yeah, you only want to deal with things within your control? Why don't you deal with this?" She gestured between the two elves. "For the love of Serra, will you two please just fuck already. I am so tired of the pining looks and having to listen to both of you whine to me about it. I'm sick of hearing about it when the one elf that I had feelings for is dead." Her voice cracked and tears began to fill her eyes, a lump rising in her throat, but she pushed them away, refusing to show weakness. She took a step back when Adri reached for her, shaking her head. "Just deal with your shit already and leave me the fuck out of it."

She didn't let the tears fall until she was locked in one of the rooms upstairs. She hadn't allowed herself to feel anything but anger towards Sinisstra whenever she had thought about her parents or Kaed. The sorrow was always there, just hidden somewhere and she couldn't reach for it until she was ready to shut down. Now, as her chest began to ache, she realized the sorrow was too much. It was going to crush her if she would let it. So she pulled two vials of a sleeping draught Gwera had made for her from her hip pouch and downed both, collapsing into the bed seconds later.

"Just when my night couldn't get worse," she grumbled to herself. Serra materialized from the darkness. "I am not in the mood for your bullshit tonight. Why didn't you just tell me everything? I had to hear it from Gwera." Serra was just another target for her anger.

"We are forbidden from interfering too much."

"Jash has already broken that so what is the point?" Serra's nostrils flared.

"Jash has played with forbidden magic. He has no idea what he has done."

"He doesn't care! He doesn't give a flying shit about what he's done because it worked! It got him what he wanted so he doesn't care about the consequences because right now he is winning." Serra nodded and took a deep breath.

"You are right." She waved a hand and Jerylia gasped as a chair formed beneath each of them. "I should have told you everything, but I did not want to overwhelm you. I am aware you already know everything but if it would make you feel better, I can tell you now."

"That would just waste more time that I don't have. Just tell me why you and Vay chose me."

"We had been making plans to choose our champions long before you were born. We each wanted to choose someone who we knew would fight for what was right and who would see through Jash's lies. Then Aselidda became pregnant. Vay and I actually fought over who would earn the right to claim you. You are descended from us both. The night you were born, I claimed you as my champion imbuing you with my power, to lie dormant until you became old enough. Vay and I were so proud. Then Jash found us and struck Vay with a death blow. Then he disappeared, laughing." Serra's lips pulled back in a snarl. "In his last moments, Vay granted his power upon you as well." Jerylia just stared at the goddess.

"So I was an accident. I was only meant to be your champion but Jash found you at just the right moment, so I ended up as a champion for both of you," she laughed, mostly to herself.

"You are not an accident." Serra reached forward and cupped her cheek. Her eyes were all intense emotion as she continued. "You are the product of a love so grand, it broke the *barrier of death."* She leaned forward until her forehead touched Jerylia's. *"You are my greatest pride, O raxo avai, kuikhdol."* I love you, daughter, *in the ancient tongue.* Jerylia swallowed the lump in her throat.

"How do I burn away my mortal body?" she asked as Serra stood and turned away from her. The goddess looked back at her and smiled softly.

"You must lose control."

Chapter 25

Theal

The squadron watched as Jerylia climbed the stairs to the second floor of the tavern, taking them two at a time, leaving them in the wake of her anger. Theal glanced at Adridia and found her avoiding his gaze. Confidence surged through him as his eyes scanned her face. These feelings weren't just going to go away and, while she didn't have to be so mean about it, Jerylia did have a point. This was something he could control so that was exactly what he was going to do. He recalled what the princess had told him in that armored carriage all those nights ago. That memory had him wrapping his fingers around Adridia's wrist and pulling her towards the stairs.

"What are you doing?" she asked, but didn't protest.

"What Jerylia told us to do: dealing with our shit." They reached the top of the stairs and entered one of the three rooms they had rented for the past few days. Adridia sat at the end of the bed and looked at anything but him. She fidgeted with her fingernails, picking at the cuticles.

"When we had been taken by the royal guard, Jerylia told me something she thought I should know, in case she didn't make it back. She told me that you had feelings for me too but never told me because you didn't want to ruin the friendship." She was quiet for a moment.

"So?" That was all she replied.

"Listen, this isn't going to work if you won't talk to me." He folded his arms over his chest. She squeezed her eyes shut for a moment.

"Okay." She took a deep breath, wiping her palms on her shift. "I don't just have feelings for you, Theal. I love you. I love your silence, your friendship, everything about you. I've loved you for years while I watched you screw your way through Serradon and instead of turning me away, it just made me love you more. You're my best friend and I didn't want to mess that up by bringing my feelings into it. I thought I was content to love you from afar but lately, something's changed and I want more." At her last words, her eyes met his and he was levelled by the intensity swirling in the amber depths. He crossed the room and sat on the bed next to her, a hand coming up to cup her cheek.

When his lips met hers, oh gods, it was more than he ever imagined. Her body molded to his like it was made to. Her lips moved against his perfectly and she tasted like the sun shining over the mountains. Her fingers slid into his hair as his other hand moved to her waist and there was no room to separate them. He wanted to stay like this forever, with her, but first, he had to tell her something. He pulled his mouth from hers and gazed into her eyes, his forehead touching hers, their chests heaving.

"I've loved you since the first moment I saw you decapitate someone." She loosed a breathless laugh. "I saw a woman so fierce and wild, I knew I wanted to be hers. I don't need you to be mine, I just want to be yours." Her eyes softened in a way he had never seen before. "I would like to activate the mating bond with you if you'll have me." She gave him a huge grin and he nearly melted. He loved her smile. He could live the rest of his days delirious just from memories of that grin. He loved every single piece of her and all those elves he'd bedded over the years could never compare to her. It would always be her. He was hers and she was his and nothing could tear her from him.

"I will have you and you can have me." Her lips met his once more. Her leg swung over his lap and his hands went to her hips, tugging her shift up. She separated from him for only a moment to pull the piece of clothing over her head, revealing her body to him. His breath caught in his lungs as inch after inch of perfect alabaster skin was exposed. She was perfect from her shoulders, thickly corded with muscle, to her stomach, with two columns of prominent abdominal muscles. She was quick to unwrap the white band around her chest, freeing her lovely breasts.

"Snap out of it." She patted his cheek gently. "Your turn." She eagerly helped him out of his tunic and loose pants. Theal moaned deep in his throat when she ran her fingers over the muscles on his abdomen, dragging them closer and closer to his very prominent erection. He closed his eyes and tilted his head back as she trailed kisses down his neck, her lips softer than he ever could have imagined. He was floored by her perfection. He put a hand on the back of her neck to pull her back up to his face before he flipped them over. Her short hair was a mess, falling over her forehead in cloudy wisps, but her eyes were glowing as he lowered his mouth to her neck, kissing and biting his way to that valley between her breasts. She moaned his name and he nearly came undone, the sound music to him. He used the knee between her legs to knock them apart, exposing her to him. Usually, foreplay was his favorite part. Giving his partner pleasure brought his own. But with the mating bond snapping into place, foreplay was unnecessary, as it usually caused completion in an instant, or so he had been told. As he slid into her, he reached inside himself, his instincts taking over. Theal knew she was doing the same thing with the way her thighs shook and her fingernails dug into his shoulder. Her teeth bit into his shoulder as her muscles contracted around him and her eyes slid shut. He found his release as the mating bond snapped into place, an overwhelming surge of emotion rolling through him with it. He groaned into her neck, his grip on her waist almost bruising. After they both caught their breath, he rolled off her, both of them sticky with sweat.

"Ten seconds, huh?" she commented, turning her head to look at him. He huffed a laugh before reaching over to brush her hair away from her face. Gods, she was beautiful and now she was his. He couldn't remember how long it had been since he'd first wanted this and now he realized he had craved this, craved her. His heart swelled with love for her as a satisfied smile stretched across her lips.

"If you are not satisfied..." he trailed off. She just smiled at him, propping herself up on one elbow so she could look him in the eyes.

"I am more than satisfied." She laid back down, this time with her head on his chest. He wrapped his arms around her and realized this was the home he had been missing. With her tucked against him, their hearts beating as one, he felt home. Theal closed his eyes and fell asleep happier than he'd been in a long time.

"You'll wake them." He woke to someone whispering somewhere in the room. He opened his eyes to see Adridia draped across him and his companions hovering around the bed, with the exception of Jerylia who stood awkwardly in the corner by the open door.

"Oh good, you're awake." Faryn grinned down at him. Adridia shifted on his chest.

"We need to go," Jerylia commented from the door.

"The grump is right. We'll meet you downstairs in ten minutes." Gwera gave a little wave as they all left. Theal smiled as he gazed down at his mate. Her eyes opened and she wrinkled her nose at him.

"Are you watching me sleep?"

"Why? Is it creepy that I am?" she snorted but didn't say anything else, just buried her face in his neck. He sighed, torn between staying like this for hours and wanting to save his country.

"We need to get up." She shook her head, clinging to his torso. "Adri." She began pressing her lips to his neck and he reached up to push her away. "You need to stop or you and I will never leave this room." She grinned and leaned in, pressing her lips to his in a searing kiss.

"I don't have a problem with that."

"Neither does Sinisstra." A frustrated groan slipped from her mouth as she pushed herself up and out of the bed.

"You had to bring her into this." She began dressing and Theal had to tear his eyes from her lovely figure.

"That and I would rather chop my own hand off than deal with an angry Gwera."

"Especially after dealing with an angry Jerylia last night. I don't know what got into her." Theal had finished dressing and was now drawing his hand through his dark hair in an attempt to tame the messy locks.

"Part of me wants to be mad at her for reacting that way but I can't. She's been through so much and on top of that, she's been acting like everything is okay just for our sake. I knew she was bottling up all of her feelings and I should have told her to take a moment and mourn but I didn't and now she's angry and stressed. I hate that she feels like she can't slow down or stop because at any moment Sinisstra could decide she no longer has a use for Aselidda. I hate that my best friend is hurting and there's not a damn thing I can do about it. I hate feeling helpless especially when it comes to Jerylia. I'm supposed to protect her but I can't protect her from this." Adridia was quiet as she spoke. She took a deep breath when she was finished as if she didn't mean for all of that to come out. "I suppose I'm so used to hiding my feelings, I never thought about how hard it actually is. Gods, I just want to pull her into a hug and hope that can keep her together long enough for us to see this through." He pulled her into his arms, resting his cheek on top of her head.

"We are all going to get through this." He felt her nod against his chest. "But not if we don't get downstairs or Gwera is going to kill us."

"That was twelve minutes." The witch was all business when they finally exited the tavern.

"Sorry, we had to throw in some morning fun." Adri winked at him.

"That explains his neck," Faryn said with a grin as Theal's hand flew to his neck. He pinned Adridia with a glare and she had the nerve to look sheepish.

It wasn't long until they were on their way to Setent. Gwera was excited to get out of the desert. She said the sand chafed her skin. Theal soared above the three women with his twin in eagle form. He looked down at Adridia, who squirmed on her ishtuk, obviously feeling the effects of the fresh mating bond. He flew lower, landing on her shoulder, careful not to pierce her skin with his talons. She smiled and reached up to run two fingers over the soft feathers on top of his head. He chirped at her, butting his head against her face before lifting himself back into the air. The sun was warm on his golden back as he danced with his twin in the air.

They reached Setent as the sun began its descent towards the horizon. The coastal city was considerably cooler than the desert towns they'd been staying in for the past weeks. Jerylia and Faryn volunteered to go find the blacksmith while the rest of them found a small tavern to hole up in while they waited. Theal and Adridia followed Gwera as she led them through the cobblestone street towards a clean white building she had been eyeing since they arrived. They took a seat at a booth in the back and ordered five bowls of whatever stew they had for the night.

"Gwera, can we ask you a favor?" Theal began as the witch pulled out her needle and asked to see the eyebrow ring Adridia had bought from Sessa.

"I'll do your mate tattoos as soon as I get her eyebrow pierced." Adri sank a little lower in her seat so Gwera could reach her face. The warrior's face pinched in pain as the needle pierced her eyebrow. Gwera whispered a few words as her eyes glowed green while she threaded the small hoop through the hole. The open space in the hoop snapped shut then glowed green for a moment before the piercing was finished.

"Give me your wrists," she told them as she pulled out her jars of ink. They both laid their wrists on the table as they pressed together, the mating bond insisting that they be touching at all times. Gwera set to work inking a small sword on his wrist and a bow with an arrow on Adridia's. She finished the delicate work and packed her needles back into her satchel as the floorboards began to rattle. Gwera paused, her eyes going wide. "We need to go."

Jerylia was in the street, screaming in the ancient tongue at anyone who would come near her and at the sky. "I'n kaavk da kdadk nav uln dul ik hak ukk, ho'k kaavk da dukdo nav nodur lavkk."

"Jer, you are not going to shove your hands up anyone's asses, that's unhygienic." Gwera attempted to calm her down. Fire blazed in the princess's eyes as she rounded on the witch.

"Then we had better get going and finish this ridiculous fucking fox hunt." She stomped her way towards the ishtuk stables, small desert cacti popping up out of the sand in her wake. Theal's eyes grew wide at the first sign of Jerylia's power awakening inside her.

"Servant of the Fae," he whispered to his mate as she looped her arm through his.

"Servant of the Fae," she repeated as they followed the one they served through the winding streets of Setent towards their next destination.

Chapter 26

Jerylia

The anger rolling off the princess was palpable. The rage hadn't dissipated in the few days since she'd allowed the emotion to take control of her completely and she was exhausted. Between the emotional toll and the uncontrolled use of her powers, she was barely keeping her eyes open. She closed her eyes for a moment, enjoying the sea breeze and the sun on her face. She felt something shift underneath her and then she was weightless before landing on the hard road. She yelped as pain lanced through her shoulder. Sand dug uncomfortably into her skin as she lay there, blinded by the sun and dazed by the fall.

"Are you okay?" Gwera was at her side in a moment, her hand wreathed in green magic, scanning her body for injuries. She sat up, clamping her jaw shut as shooting pain shot down her arm from her shoulder.

"I'm fine." She gritted her teeth together as she attempted to stand. Black spots appeared in her vision as her shoulder shifted, forcing her back to the ground. She sighed in defeat. "No, my shoulder." Gwera brought her hands to the shoulder in question, careful not to touch it.

"Just a dislocation."

"I know what a dislocation feels like, it's happened before. Just fix it." Gwera pressed her lips together and grasped Jerylia's hand, tugging hard to pop the joint back into place. She felt the bones snap back together and yelped at the sudden pain. Gwera tugged a long strip of fabric out of her satchel and tied it around Jerylia's neck, tucking her arm into it.

"You and I are going to ride together and you are going to sleep." Jerylia shook her head.

"No, I'm fine." Gwera put both hands on her cheeks and forced her to look into her eyes. Her almost white irises swirled with concern.

"No, you're not. This is not up for debate. This is me telling you that we are riding together and you are going to rest. I know the toll untrained powers can take on your body and your mortal body is not powerful enough to withstand the powers of a goddess." The witch was right. She could feel the well of power inside of her. Her anger had caused it to spill over and the rogue desert plants had just been the surface of what she could do but she was afraid to look too deep into the well, afraid of what she might do if she reached for more power than she could control. The power felt familiar, so much like her mother's, she wanted to wrap herself in it just to feel close to the queen again. But there was also something wild, uncontrolled in the well. She could feel its hunger there, lingering beneath the power of life and it scared her.

"I can't sleep, Gwere." The witch helped her stand. "Serra doesn't allow me to rest." Gwera's eyes softened.

"You are one of her daughters, Jer. Allow her to visit one last time." Jerylia nodded before climbing back onto the ishtuk, Gwera pulling herself up behind her. It wasn't long before her eyes slid shut and she found herself in the fog heavy realm of her dreams.

"My child." Serra's smile was warm as she pulled the princess into a hug. *"This is the last I will be seeing you."* She

pulled away and Jerylia gasped. Wrinkles spread from the corners of her eyes and mouth. Her once luscious hair was now completely streaked through with grey and her back bowed slightly.

"What happened?"

"You used my power, thus taking the last of what was keeping me alive." Serra didn't seem saddened by that fact. She seemed content and at peace with what was happening to her.

"I don't know what to say."

"You don't have to say anything, child." Serra reached out a hand and patted her cheek softly. "I will be with the rest of my daughters and my love. It's been a long twenty-six years without him." She folded Jerylia's hands into her gnarled ones. "It is your turn to take up the mantle, my dear. Bear my name with yours and make them remember you long after you fade."

"When will I fade?" In truth, she had been dreading life as an immortal. After a certain number of millennia, being alive becomes disinteresting and that's why many fae lives ended in suicide after too many years of being alive. It was the thing she dreaded the most about becoming Fae, and her mating bond, chosen by fate.

"You don't have to worry about that for a long time yet. But you cannot rule for your entire lifetime. Give up your throne when your children come of age. Find a way to keep life interesting. I would hate to see you end up like so many Fae I knew. Or worse, like Jash, who allowed the darkness to grow with his boredom." A figure, wreathed in light appeared in the distance. It held out its hand and Serra smiled. "It appears my time has come to an end. Yai varr urvuavk ko nav klaikokd nanovd." A tear slid down Jerylia's cheek at her last sentence. 'You will always be my proudest moment.'

The goddess stepped away from the princess towards the figure of light. It folded her into its arms and leaned down for a kiss. There was a bright flash and they were gone.

Jerylia woke with a start, blinking the sleep from her eyes.

"You have impeccable timing. We're almost to Myard." Gwera spoke from behind her. Jerylia turned to look at the witch and she gasped. "Your eyes are glowing."

"Serra is gone. I took the last of her power. Which means Jash might be the only god left alive if the rest of them have given up their powers."

"Which means we have a huge problem. Jash has had millennia to hone his powers and grow them. You may have the powers of two gods inside of you but you won't have the kind of control required to wield them properly."

Jerylia was quiet. The anger was quickly returning. She felt powerless. Powerless to save her mother, powerless against Sinisstra, and powerless in this never-ending fox hunt to find the dragonslayer. It was burning, writhing inside of her. The instant they reached the city limits she slid off her ishtuk and lashed out at the first person she saw. He was terrified as she grabbed the front of his shirt and pulled him close enough to speak to him.

"Where can I find Terrar?" His eyes widened as a date palm sprung up behind her, the ground vibrating under their feet.

"T-the temple," he managed to get out.

"Which temple?"

"Of Della." He pointed across the city to a grand temple towering high above everything else. She let go of his shirt and he fell to the ground, scrambling away from her as she muttered her thanks.

The temple was beautiful. The exterior was made from sandstone, the different colors creating stripes across the grand columns that stood guard in front of the entrance. The doorways had no doors, nothing that could block the path of someone seeking Della's help. The interior was made of the same sandstone with accents of bronze along the walls and floors. The moment they stepped foot into the temple, an acolyte dressed in a thin grey robe greeted them. She noticed the mark of Della tattooed on his forehead, in between his eyebrows.

"Hello, travelers. How can we serve you?"

"We're looking for Terrar," Jerylia said in Hrinthian. The acolyte smiled and led them to a side room with a map carved into the sandstone floor, the names of the cities inlaid with bronze. An elderly priest in the same grey robes knelt in front of a statue at the head of the room. She wore a more traditional shift, one typically made from a large square of fabric with holes cut along the fold and a rope tied around the waist. It fell along the body, accentuating curves with its many creases. It was very popular to wear in warmer climates before more advanced methods of making clothes were developed. Her arms were stretched wide, the fabric of her shift creating a haunting silhouette. From the waist down, the cloth clung to her skin, looking as if it was being blown behind her and her hair, which had been carved with great care, flowed behind her and down her back. One carefully carved leg stuck out of the shift, a snake wrapped around her thigh. Her face was severe yet gentle in the eyes. The artist who carved this must have held a great passion for their goddess.

"Terrar?" The man stood and faced them, his arms tucked into his sleeves. "We're looking for Caerin Ocealith. We were told you might be able to tell us where we could find him."

Terrar said nothing as he shuffled across the floor and sat, cross-legged, on the carved map. She opened her mouth to scream, to shout, to do anything to let out the rage swelling in her chest when her eyes fell to the right of the elder. 'Greydell' was carved into the floor just next to him along with a clear path through the mountains. It would be dangerous and exhausting but it was the only way. The princess knelt so she could look Terrar in the eye while Gwera scrambled to find her map.

"Thank you." She could cry from the relief that swept through her at finally having a location.

"I must warn you, child. His mind will not be what it once was. It has been a hundred years since he stole away to the mountains with his dragons." She nodded and thanked him once more before leaving the temple.

Jerylia's anger was soon replaced with excitement as they headed in the direction of the mountains. She was eager to reach their destination because it meant she was one step closer to bashing Sinisstra's face in.

Chapter 27

Jerylia

The anger was gone. Jerylia tilted her face towards the wind and breathed in deeply. She could see the mountains looming in the distance and felt drawn to them, like a rope around her waist pulling her closer with every second. The desert slowly gave way to a lush forest, teeming with life. She could feel it pulsing through the air around her, coaxing the magic from her veins. She reached out and brushed her fingers over the curling petals of a white flower. Four more sprouted around it and she laughed, the sound ringing through the trees around them. She closed her eyes and breathed in deeply, feeling the song of life vibrating through her. She could feel the humming in her very bones and with her eyes closed, she could almost feel her mother with her there, guiding the song through her. When she finally opened her eyes, Gwera was watching her closely with an eyebrow raised.

"We can stop here for the night." She slid off her ishtuk and swatted its rear flank. It took off running in the direction they came from. "These birds won't do well in this environment. They need to go home." The rest of them did the same thing and began making a camp. Theal and Adridia offered to go find firewood, though their laced hands told the rest of them it would take longer than necessary. Faryn offered to find dinner and took off into the brush.

"You aren't doing anything," Gwera told her when she

opened her mouth, eager to help to atone for her bad attitude over the past couple of days. "You are going to stay here and control yourself. Sit." Jerylia reluctantly did as she was told. "Close your eyes and reach inside yourself. Find your power and make it obey you. You are its master. You control it. It does not control you."

So she closed her eyes and reached for that well of power. It was wild, raw and it wanted to escape but she told it no. She repeated what Gwera had said, directing her will into it. She was its master and it would obey her. She skimmed some off the top and let it flow through her but never out of her. It filled her veins, her fingertips tingling from the sensation. It wanted out but she couldn't let it out, not until she knew she could control it. So she sat there and let it roil inside of her but it wouldn't dissipate. Power must be transferred because it cannot be destroyed or created. The energy must come from somewhere and go somewhere.

"Where does it go, Gwera?" She opened her eyes to see Gwera leaning against a tree. The witch looked up at the leafless branches.

"This tree is dying. See if you can help it live." She pushed herself off the tree and Jerylia stood, stepping forward, laying her hands flat on the trunk. She closed her eyes and pulled that power forward, pushing it into the tree. She pulled away quickly when the tree answered her magic. It was faint but there was a pulse of energy pushing against her, not pushing her away, just letting her know that there was life in this tree yet. She put her hands back on the trunk and pushed the rest of that stagnant magic into the tree and she watched as leaves sprouted on the branches, the tree bursting into full bloom. That pulse of life within grew stronger, whispering into her very soul, thanking her for the gift. "You are amazing, Little Serra." Gwera watched her with awe.

A growl ripped through the clearing. The women turned to find a large wolf snarling at them. Two more appeared on either side of them and they could see eyes reflecting in the shadows of the trees. Jerylia eyed her sword, gently placed on top of her pack. If she was quick enough, she could grab it and draw it before the wolves could do any damage. Her spine stiffened as she felt that call, that invisible line snapping in place between her and the snarling animal. A sense of calm settled over her as she realized the sword was not the answer. She sent a whisper of magic flickering over it and the wolf stopped growling and sat back on its haunches, tilting its head to the side in a questioning sort of way.

"What did you do?" Gwera whispered.

"I have no idea," she whispered back as she crept forward, staying low so as to not frighten the poor beast. She held out a hand as she neared it and the wolf's nose twitched as it leaned forward and sniffed. Its tongue flashed out to lick her hand before it howled once and disappeared into the dark of the forest. "What the hell just happened?" She looked down at her hands as if they could tell her the answer.

"You are descended from the goddess of life, my dear. You are connected to all life." They both jumped as Adridia and Theal crashed into the clearing, both laden with branches. Theal had a ridiculous smile on his face and a fresh bruise on his neck. Jerylia smiled at her friends, her family. They had finally found happiness within each other and some small part of her was just the tiniest bit smug that it was her that had finally forced them together. She laid out her bedroll near where Adridia was building the fire and stretched out on it, sighing at the pull in her spine as it relaxed, the tense muscles in her back loosening.

"So, Jer, have you made a plan to win the Dragonslayer's

favor?" Theal asked from his own bedroll.

"I told you, before, I'm just going to let my charm take care of that," she grinned.

"How is that going to work?" she smirked and stood, undoing the top laces on her tunic to show her generous cleavage and sweeping her cloak to the side, showing off the roundness of her ass.

"I'll use my assets," Adridia laughed.

"It works. That's all I had to do. As soon as Theal saw my tits he was locked in." Adridia followed Jerylia's example, unlacing the front of her shirt. Theal's eyes were unmistakably drawn to her chest and he quickly clenched his jaw and looked away.

"Don't involve me in this," he protested, earning laughs from the rest of them.

"Having fun without me?" Faryn strode into the clearing with several birds hanging from his neck. They were round, most likely ground birds, with white feathers, spotted with black.

"Usually," Gwera commented as Adridia finally lit the fire. Heat washed over Jerylia and she closed her eyes, relishing in the warmth.

"I actually wanted to know if we were going to take the bribery route or if we were going to be able to convince him that it's the right thing to do." Jerylia plopped back down on her bedroll.

"Well, with one of Gwera's special potions, I figured we could make him do just about anything." She glanced at the witch hopefully.

"Nice try. We are going to do this honestly, and not just because I don't have the ingredients out here. Because Caerin could be a powerful ally not just in this war but also in future wars."

"I hate it when you're right." She folded her arms over her chest and watched the twins pluck the birds that were to be their dinner.

"Then you must hate me all the time." Gwera smiled brightly and moved to sit next to Jerylia. "I'm going to change your face again."

"But I like this face." Gwera placed her hands on Jerylia's cheeks and began whispering in the ancient tongue. Her skin tingled as it turned from the slate grey color she had grown used to back to her Serradonian hue, almost as white as the snow with a pink tinge to her cheeks from the chilled air.

"You have another change coming, don't worry. Your Fae face will look different, more regal than this one."

"Are you saying I don't look regal?"

"I am not, now stop trying to start something."

"Did Serra ever tell you how to lose your mortal body?" Theal asked from his spot next to his mate.

"She told me I had to lose control, which, if the other half of my powers are from Vay, those are sun powers. I'd rather not burn the forest down."

"This is a very dull conversation," Faryn interjected as he ripped his birds into easily cookable pieces. "We should be celebrating. We know where the Dragonslayer is. While our goal is still pretty far away, at least we're one step closer than we were a few days ago." Jerylia smiled. Faryn had been acting strange ever since she was taken by the king. Perhaps he had felt guilty about her being taken or maybe he was feeling remorse for that night before her wedding. Gods, it seemed like forever ago. Things between them were different now. Before she felt like she needed to avoid his gaze, never be left alone with him and there was always this strange tension between them. He was one of her oldest friends but for the past few years, she had grown to dislike him, his habit of using women something she could never agree with. He had turned into the worst kind of an ass. Now, when she looked at him, she felt nothing but a brotherly fondness for him. He smiled back at her and she easily met his gaze, their friendship from before the complication falling into place between them. Somehow, during this horrible yet beautiful adventure, he had fallen out of love with her. So she stood, raising her skin of water.

"Faryn is right. Gwera, turn this water to wine so we may dance beneath the stars." She held it towards the witch who only sat with her arms folded over her chest, making no effort to move from her position.

"Yeah, I can't do that." Jerylia retracted the skin.

"What do you mean you can't do that? You can turn coppers to gold."

"You're asking me to change water into grape juice and then that juice into a fermented form. I can't even begin to try to explain that science to you or why I can't accomplish it in just one night. Coppers are already metal, so changing them to gold doesn't take much power. To change water to wine would take at least seven spells and I'm exhausted from maintaining my bottomless satchel for weeks and changing you."

"Gwere, you're making me look bad," the witch sighed and reached into her satchel to pull out a bottle of wine. Jerylia cheered and snatched the bottle from her. She used her dagger to wedge the cork out before taking a deep drink. "What vintage is this?"

"I just pulled it out of a satchel, hell if I know." Gwera took the bottle from her and drank.

"How about a song from our illustrious Fae queen." Adridia

raised the bottle and the rest of them whooped their agreement. Jerylia smiled, the alcohol warming her cheeks.

"*I get on with life as a queen, I'm a powerful kind of person.*" Faryn began patting his legs like drums and Theal brought his hands to his mouth to whistle the tune. "*I like drinking and fighting and handling swords.*" Gwera chimed in with harmony. "*But when I start to daydream, my mind turns straight to wine.*"

"*Oh, oh, oh,*" Adridia belted.

"*Do I love wine more than swords? Do I love wine more than swords?*" Jerylia sat back down beside Gwera when the forest began swaying and wrapped her arm around the smaller elf's shoulder. "*I like to use words about swords, but when I stop talking, my mind turns straight to wine. Do I love wine more than swords? Do I love wine more than swords?*" The last word was held out for a comically long note that came from deep in the throat and always ended with a laugh, as all bar songs do. Soon, the five companions were laughing around the fire as they enjoyed the roasted birds caught by the twins.

"I would like to propose a toast." Faryn held the bottle and stood, his eyes meeting Jerylia's. "I would like to formally apologize for being an ass to you the night before your wedding. I would also like to express my deepest condolences to you about your father and husband-to-be. You have a huge heart, Jer, and you fill it with people and things that you love. You filled it with us and your parents and sharp metal objects and snow flowers. Theal and I have watched you grow up and we grew up with you. You've grown into a powerful young woman and will continue to grow into a powerful queen. We have all had the privilege of watching you change into different people over the years as you learned the world around you, as you filled up your heart with people and things. And your mother is the luckiest person in the world right now, even if she is a prisoner in her own kingdom because she doesn't have to worry about not being rescued. She knows that she has you coming for her and that one day, you'll come home. I know I've been a pain in the ass for all of you, with my sex stories and just general shitty behavior, but you stayed by my side and I would like to thank you all for that." Tears were welling in Jerylia's eyes as he sat back down.

"Shit, there's something in my eyes." Adridia ducked her head behind her hand.

"Those are tears, bitch." Jerylia let them flow as she stood to walk over to Faryn. He seemed taken aback when she wrapped her arms around him. "You will always have a place in my heart." He hugged her back for a moment, a few of his tears wetting her hair before they parted and Jerylia returned to her bedroll.

"You guys are my only family. My mother died a few years ago and most of my extended family don't acknowledge that I exist because I'm a witch. I don't know what would have happened to me if I did not have you when my mother died. I love each of you and I always will no matter what happens during this war." Gwera wiped at her cheeks.

"All this mushy shit has got to stop. I haven't cried this much ever." Adridia fanned her face and Theal wrapped an arm around her broad shoulders.

"I think it's time for sleep." Jerylia was beginning to struggle to keep her eyes open, exhaustion tugging at her limbs. Gwera moved to her own bedroll and the princess laid down, wrapping herself in her thick cloak.

She slept peacefully for the first night in weeks.

Chapter 28

Faryn

Serradon was a very mountainous country. The southern border was flatlands good for farming and the western coast had flat beaches but the rest of the country was famous for its mountains. Faryn was no stranger to grueling hikes over treacherous mountain paths and snow. But this was just torture. The air was chilled, flushing his cheeks and nose, but the physical exertion coupled with the thick layers he was wearing made him sweat, which soon soaked through his first layer. He shivered, torn between pulling his cloak tighter around himself and opening it to let his clothing dry. But no matter how hard he tried, he couldn't bring himself to be miserable. All he could think of was home and just how close they were to their goal. There was an aura of excitement around the five companions as they hiked in almost silence, most of them lost in their own thoughts.

"Do we know how long it's going to take to get through to the valley?" he called up to Gwera, who had the map and had taken it upon herself to lead the way.

"A few days. There are a few spots that will require careful maneuvering," Faryn groaned and pushed forward.

"Oh, my gods!" Jerylia shouted. Faryn looked up to see fat snowflakes falling from the sky. He paused in his trek to watch them float lazily to the ground. "I forgot how much I love a northern spring," she squealed in excitement and held her hands up to try to catch the flakes to watch them melt against her skin. Her smile was infectious and he found himself matching it with one of his own.

His chest began to ache as he looked around them. Pines rose above them, their sharp scent surrounding them. The sky was covered by gray clouds. It hit him that he missed his home. They'd been gone for a little over a month and he'd been able to avoid thinking about the pine forests and frozen lakes of their homeland. He missed the stone castle, his haven for almost twenty years. He missed Serramor, that beautiful capital city that hosted most of his mischief. He was brought out of his homesickness by a squeal of delight. Jerylia dropped to the ground.

"It's a snow flower." Her fingers brushed the red petals and he was reminded of how much the princess adored them. They were a symbol of her kingdom, a reminder of home. The queen had filled the royal gardens with them because her only daughter had requested it. She closed her eyes and suddenly, the red flowers were sprouting all around us, a field of crimson.

"It's beautiful, Jer." Gwera was in awe of the princess' power.

"Let's keep going." Jerylia's cerulean eyes grew sad and Faryn knew she was thinking of her mother, trapped in her own home.

They climbed in silence for hours. The short mountain grass eventually gave way to thick snow as they climbed higher and higher. Stony peaks rose up around them and one step in the wrong place could mean instant death. Faryn was still sweating but the air was growing colder and soon they could all see their breath. His cheeks and nose were frozen as he pulled his fur-lined hood over his head and clasped the front of his cloak shut to keep out the icy wind. He found his thoughts drifting like the snow around them.

"Gwera, we need to stop for the night. I can't feel my fingers anymore." Jerylia's whole body was shaking. Faryn stepped up next to her and wrapped an arm around her, sharing his body heat. She looked up at him and grinned. Her hands were inside his hood in a flash, her frozen fingers on his neck. He made a strangled noise and pulled away from her quickly, the ghost of her icy hands on his skin.

"Yeah, we need to stop." He pulled his hood tighter as Jerylia howled with laughter. Gwera knelt in the snow, a ghost of a smile on her face. She opened her satchel in front of her and flicked her fingers through the air, whispering under her breath. Green wisps of magic speared through the air with bolts of canvas and metal rods. Soon two tents were set up perfectly.

"Jerylia, I need your help with fuel for a fire." The witch led the princess over to a tree. "You know you can push life into a tree but you can also pull life from it. We can't burn a living tree but we can burn a dead one." Jerylia nodded and placed her palms on the trunk, closing her eyes. The pine needles began to turn brown and fell around her, slowly. Her brow pinched and she retracted her hands with a hiss. "It's not enough," Gwera told her.

"I can't, Gwere. It's in so much pain." A tear traced down her cheek. Gwera nodded in understanding.

"You have to." Jerylia squared her shoulders and took a deep breath, placing her palms on the trunk again. More tears followed the first as more needles fell from its branches.

"I can't watch this." Adridia turned away as Jerylia began to scream. Gwera's eyes were sad as she watched their princess and swiped one of her palms over the other as she whispered a spell. The last of the needles fell and the princess stopped screaming as

Gwera placed her hands flat against each other and made a sweeping motion. The tree fell into a pile of burnable logs. Jerylia scrambled back, wiping her cheeks.

"Don't ever make me do that again." Adridia pulled her into a tight embrace as Faryn moved forward to help the witch set up a fire.

"Did you really have to make her do that?" he asked her as they stacked the logs.

"She's barely scratched the surface of her power and her mortal body is holding her back. She needs to understand what she is capable of and accept it, sooner rather than later." He suddenly understood why Gwera was here. She was their driving force. Jerylia saw something in her and had invited her into their squadron but he had never understood exactly why, besides the fact that having a witch around is very handy. Gwera was compassionate but hardened by her world. She knew what had to be done and how to get it done, no matter the cost. They finished stacking a portion of the logs into a nice cube shape and Gwera snapped her fingers over the pile. There was a flash of green then orange flames were licking at the wood.

Soon they sat around the fire, all huddled in their cloaks, silent as they listened to the sounds of the mountains. Jerylia stared at the flames, an uneaten piece of dried meat dangling from her fingers. A sudden roar shook the trees around them, echoing off the stone. Faryn had his bow out in a flash and was on his feet, ready for whatever made that sound. A shadow passed overhead and another roar shook the earth. His mouth fell open as a massive dragon landed just a few yards from their camp, snow spraying under its feet. It was a beautiful shade of white, its scales shining from the firelight. It crouched on four legs and tucked its wings into its body. It snarled at them, massive teeth glinting from a huge maw. He drew back the string of his bow as Jerylia pushed forward and held her hands out.

"Hold on." He lowered his weapon as she got low, slowly making her way towards the beast. "You're not going to hurt us." She spoke softly as if it was a dog to be soothed. The snarling stopped and it titled its head, trying to figure out what she was doing. She held a hand out and it sniffed her before pressing its nose to her palm. Jerylia breathed a sigh of relief and ran her hand over its snout. It made a vibrating noise, almost like a purr and Jerylia laughed. Her eyes widened suddenly and she whispered to it, "Hadi." The beast withdrew its head and shot into the sky, blasting us with wind.

"What the absolute hell was that?" Adridia was still staring at the sky as if she could see where it went. "What did you say to it?"

"Hadi, it's her name." Jerylia's legs were shaking as she came closer to the fire. "I think I need to lie down." Then she was falling over, straight into the snow.

Chapter 29

Jerylia

The princess woke in a bed, in her bedroom in Serramor. Her mother burst into the room, handmaidens at her side.

"Get up, darling." She rolled over as her mother sat on the edge of her bed, picking up the book that had kept Jerylia occupied until the small hours of the morning.

"Or I could keep sleeping." The queen's laugh was musical as she pulled the blankets away from her daughter's body.

"But it is Serralas and we leave for the summer palace in two days." The queen strode over to the windows and yanked the heavy curtains back to let the sunshine in. The princess groaned and sat up in her bed. She allowed her mother to pull her from the soft sheets and the handmaidens to prepare her for the festival and then the evening ball. They dressed her in a silver dress with a high collar and long sleeves with a hem that reached her calves embroidered with black flowers under a black armored corset matched with a pair of tall, black leather boots. They left her hair wild and wavy with a pair of tight braids on the side of her head decorated with silver rings and cuffs.

"Foebreaker!" Adridia had shouted when they met up in the town square for the midday activities. A stage was set up near the grand marble fountain with the triplet goddesses standing together in the center, the water pouring from their outstretched hands. Actors depicting different warrior queens through the ages pranced across it. Booths were set up on the edges of the square offering delicacies, toys, and games. "I can't believe your mother stuffed you into that." Jerylia glanced down at her dress and rolled her eyes.

"I am first and foremost a princess, Adri," she reminded her.

"My heart!" Adridia slipped away as her mother approached, linking her elbow with her daughter's. Her father was with the queen, standing back a pace as they moved through the crowd, Serradonians of all ages stopping to greet them with joyous smiles on their faces. Happiness swelled in her chest as she strolled with her mother. "This will all be yours someday." The words echoed into darkness as the memory slipped away. Jerylia was falling, falling, falling into nothing. Then she was caught by another memory.

"I cannot believe I caught you with that boy in the kitchens!" She had never seen her mother so angry. The queen had caught her sharing kisses with the cute cook's apprentice. He had been her first at sixteen and she'd had to lie to him about who she was since no one was willing to take the princess' virtue.

"I wanted to know what it felt like, Mother!" she had yelled back. "Faryn and Theal have done that and more and they constantly talk about it and I just wanted to know what it felt like to be wanted in that way." The queen's eyes had softened as she pulled Jerylia into an embrace, a hand smoothing her hair.

"I'm sorry, my heart." A tear rolled down her cheek.

"Why did I have to be born the only elf in the country who can't be normal?" Aselidda closed her eyes and breathed in through her nose.

"You were meant for so much. Your virtue is valuable as are you. You are my only child and I love you with everything I have and everything I am. I get a little protective at times and I know you wish more than anything to be normal but Serra chose you for more. She chose you to protect the people of her and her sisters. I never needed another child when I had you, but if you sincerely wish for it, you can step down from your position as the crown princess. You can have a normal life, you can do normal things. You did not ask for the burden you were born with and so I cannot force it upon you." Jerylia shook her head and pulled away from her mother, wiping away her tears.

"I could not ask that of you. I am a descendant of Serra. I will suffer any challenge that is sent my way." Her mother smiled and brushed her hair behind her ear.

"You are right about that." Her eyes grew stern. "I don't ever want to catch you with another boy. You cannot afford the freedoms your two companions take." Jerylia chuckled at the distaste in her mother's voice. The door to the queen's chamber burst open and her father rushed in, a murderous look in his eyes.

"I heard there was a boy," Aselidda chuckled and stood.

"You can handle him, dear," Jerylia began to protest as her mother left the room.

Her father rounded on her but before he could speak she was falling once again.

Jerylia crept along the high stone towers of the mountain palace in Eowessmor. She was dressed in all black with her hair braided down her back. She spotted her mother's profile through one of the stained glass windows. The sun was setting and the queen would be meeting her father in their private chambers for a small dinner. Her final task to complete her assassin's training was to sneak up on her mother without being noticed. She climbed the tower that housed the queen's quarters and slid in through the iron paned window of the bathroom. Her slippers were silent on the marble floor as she crept into the bedroom. She could hear her parents talking from the adjoining dining room. She rolled to the doorway and leaned against the wall next to the frame, inhaling silently. Her eyes snapped open when her mother's voice grew louder.

"There's enough here for you if you would like some, my heart." Her heart fell and she stood, entering the dining room.

"How did you know I was there?" Her mother smiled and shook her head as the princess made herself a plate. She smiled at her father as he slid an extra sweet roll towards her.

"Darling, the bathroom window pane is made of iron that squeaks when it is breathed on too heavily. Perhaps next time, try to be in the room before I enter or catch me unsuspecting in the halls."

"I was so excited to be done with the assassin training. What am I training for next?" Aselidda smiled softly at her daughter.

"I have arranged for a master of hand-to-hand combat to come train you, but that won't be until you complete your assassin's training." Jerylia sighed and shoved a forkful of potatoes into her mouth.

"You have so much time to complete all of your training, baby." Her father placed a comforting hand on her shoulder and she smiled at him, contentment settling in her stomach.

She fell again, landing in her worst memory. Her father nudged her forward as they approached the queen, lying in her bed. The healers bowed as they left the room, carrying bloodied sheets in their arms. Aselidda's eyes were closed and sweat shone on her forehead. She shifted and her eyes opened, just a crack. Her hand fell over the side of the bed, reaching for her daughter.

"Come here, my heart." Jerylia shuffled forward on tiny feet. "Remember how we talked about you being a big sister?" Jerylia only nodded, dread settling in her stomach.

"You had a brother. He was beautiful." Her mother smoothed her hair away from her face. "He looked just like you."

"Momma, I thought he wasn't going to be here until the second week of Kendiel." Her mother smiled softly, her eyes filling with tears.

"You're right, my heart. But he decided he wanted to see the world a little early." Aselidda closed her eyes and rested her forehead against Jerylia's. "He only cried once before he went to be with Serra." Jerylia suddenly understood her mother's grief as her own tears began to fall. Her father climbed into bed beside them and held her mother, Jerylia wedged between them, and they mourned their loss together as a family.

Then she wasn't in a memory anymore. She was in a cell in her own castle. A woman lay crumpled on the floor, absolutely defeated. Two guards came in and grabbed the woman, lifting her by her arms. Jerylia gasped when she realized it was her mother. She reached for her, stumbling when her hands glided through the queen's arms as if they were nothing but air, an illusion. But this wasn't an illusion, it couldn't be. It felt too real. She pulled her hands back and looked at them. She wasn't here, not really, but where and when exactly was here? She followed the guards to her mother's throne room and collapsed to her knees at what she saw. The hole in the ceiling had been fixed but her mother's throne and Jerylia's had been smashed to rubble. The intricate carvings lay in pieces around where they once stood and a grand white throne rose up in its place. Jerylia looked closer and realized the white rods that made up the new throne were elven bones and fought the urge to vomit. A huge wyvern with scales of deep red and metallic grey wrapped around the base of the throne, snoozing. A tall woman with inky black locks dressed in a silk black gown with a plunging neckline and two slits that rose all the way up to her hips lounged on the throne. She wore a glittering black crown and her lips were painted a deep red. She smiled darkly, elongated canines flashing in the torchlight.

"Welcome to my new throne room, Aselidda," she mocked as she brought a glass full of red wine to her lips. "I hope you like what I've done with the place."

"I've been wondering when our next torture session would be," Aselidda ground out from her place on the floor. She would never allow Sinisstra to see how weak she was but Jerylia saw her arms shake as she pushed herself to a sitting position.

"Oh, there won't be a torture session." Sinisstra stood and strode down the steps. She knelt in front of the queen and gripped her jaw with a firm hand. "Your people will never accept me the way they have accepted you as their queen, which I should have foreseen. I have to hand it to you Serradonians, it was crafty what you did. You created an entire religion around your lineage sitting *their* ass in this throne. How can I compare to the descendant of a goddess? And not just any goddess, the almighty Serra, protector of the throne." Sinisstra's voice dripped with venom. "Mercy is not a kindness I can afford. I am going to kill you and then I will find your brat of a daughter and I will kill her too. Cordava will be mine to rule and mine alone." Her voice had grown darker, deeper, and there was an edge to it, almost like a shovel sliding over gravel. Aselidda lurched as a bejeweled dagger was shoved between her ribs, a slow painful death that ended with the victim drowning in their own blood. Sinisstra stood and Jerylia screamed. Her mother's eyes found hers as the life faded from them, that tenuous string holding her in that spot between life and death.

"I will always be with you, my heart," she whispered before the last breath left her body.

Jerylia woke screaming, unable to catch her breath. Adridia had her arms around the princess within moments, trying to calm her. She turned to see Gwera hovering over her bedroll with shaking hands, her eyes still glowing green.

"What the fuck did you do to me?" she screamed at the witch as she scrambled to her feet, tears pouring from her eyes. Gwera looked up at her, hollow.

"I had no idea you would see that, Jer. I'm so sorry." Jerylia shoved away from Adridia and stumbled out of the tent, her companions following her. Hysteric tears slid down her cheeks as she fought to catch her breath, fought to stay alive with this pain in her chest. Oh, gods, it hurt. It felt like someone was slowly squeezing her heart and she didn't see an end to it. "Jerylia, please, it was the only way to see what was happening back home." Gwera grabbed at her arms.

"I just watched my mother die, Gwera." She pushed the witch back, Faryn catching the petite elf. "Risk your own heart next time." She stumbled away from the camp, wiping furiously at the tears that poured from her eyes. She didn't know where she was going, only that she needed to put distance between herself and the witch before she did something she would regret. Her companions attempted to follow but Gwera held them back, shaking her head slightly.

The princess fell to her knees in a circle of pines and let out a soul-shattering scream filled with anguish deeper than the sea. She felt that well of power inside of her boiling over but there was nothing she could do about it as it consumed her, filled every cell in her body until she was glowing with it, that beautiful and deadly power that belonged to her mother. Her mother, her heart, the queen, the only blood family she had left in this world, gone in a heartbeat, just like that. And Jerylia had to watch, unable to interfere, unable to help, unable to do *anything*. Because of Gwera, her friend that she loved. The betrayal rocked through her, shattering what was left of her resolve.

Her back arched and she threw her head back, arms outstretched as the power became too much. She needed to let it go before it destroyed her but she was lost in her grief. Her grief for her mother, her father, her foreign prince. The list of people she had loved and then lost was growing. She screamed again as pain ripped through her. Oh, gods, it was tearing her apart. Light cracked through her skin. She curled in on herself as patches of her skin began to burn. Ivy burst from her leg, shooting through her skin and wrapping around her as it turned black and squeezed. She felt something sprout from her back and turned to see a tall white flower spearing from her skin. She had become a slave to the power inside of her and now it was going to kill her. Her head tilted back and she looked up to the sky, praying that her mother could see her, that she knew her daughter was coming to be with her forever.

"No." She whipped around to see her mother standing there, regal as ever with a silver glow around her. "You cannot join me, my heart."

"I miss you," she sobbed, then groaned with pain as a snow flower sprouted from her shoulder. "I can't do this, momma. It hurts so much." The pain was consuming her, occupying her every thought. She could feel the darkness reaching for her. She wanted to submit, succumb, forget everything. Aselidda smiled and stepped forward, resting a soft hand on her cheek.

"Then let go." The words echoed around her as the queen disappeared. She closed her eyes and breathed in deep, allowing the grief and the sorrow and the anger to swallow her for only a moment more. Then she let it all go.

Her face tilted towards the sky as she felt her skin burn away. Greenery sprouted all around her before wave after wave of white-hot flames burned it all to ash in an instant. The mountain air was still around her as she stood on shaking legs. The snow had completely melted in a perfect circle around her and the trees had burned away. She caught a glimpse of herself in a puddle and stumbled back, falling into the mud.

She didn't even look like herself anymore. For starters, she was tall. Taller than the Kaen twins. That extra layer of stomach and thigh fat she had always tried to get rid of was gone, leaving toned muscle in its place. Her cheekbones were sharper and her jawline could cut glass. Her eyes were the same blue they had always been but they were deeper, more reflective, with a certain sparkle. Her hair still held its signature waves but the color was more vibrant and it was silkier, less frizzy. Her ears were still pointed but they were longer and when she opened her mouth, elongated canines appeared behind her lips. On top of all of that, she had an air of superiority around her, a glow to her skin that said she was not like the elves around her. She was something more. A chill spread over her and she realized she was naked, her skin had burned away along with her clothes, though the ink embedded in her skin was still intact, probably through the magic of the tattooists.

"Holy fuck." Adridia entered the clearing, Jerylia's cloak folded over her arm. She draped it over the princess, no, the queen before stepping back, her mouth falling open.

"Harav Serra, vo dano hinkrav da avail dhlavo uvk kav da avail dhakov tioov." Gwera stumbled into the clearing and immediately threw herself to the ground at her feet.

"My queen." Theal and Faryn knelt before her as she stood, barefoot in the frozen mud.

Chapter 30

Jerylia

The five companions travelled in silence through the mountain path. Jerylia refused to speak to Gwera after what she had done to her. Theal and Adridia traded hushed whispers back and forth, something that was beginning to wear on Jerylia's last nerve. She was already five seconds away from snapping and burning down the entire mountain forest because her clothes no longer fit her and she was forced to wear a pair of Theal's leggings which fit very snugly over her new legs and one of Faryn's tunics which was made for a man so the neckline dipped lower than her usual tunics. She was constantly adjusting it so her breasts wouldn't fall out.

She stopped suddenly as they emerged from between two shale cliffs onto a shelf overlooking an open valley. Her eyes scanned the scene before her, awe filling her veins.

An ancient castle rose up on the easternmost side of the valley, the stone structure nestled against the cliff. The valley was lush and green, covered in a thin layer of fog. From her position on the shelf, she could see a small farm and a cattle pen. But what shocked her the most was the sheer amount of dragons roaming free around the valley. Dragons of all colors and sizes nested down there. She could see several different types, all grouped within their kind. Dragons, wyverns, wyrms, amphitheres, lindwurms, and even a mated pair of drakes took up residence.

She squinted at the small mop of wine red hair that exited the castle, her new fae eyes assisting her. She gasped, taking a small step back when she realized that Caerin had emerged into his fae form. He looked to be tall, taller than even her new fae form. She could tell he lived alone here with nothing to do from his broad shoulders and arms that rippled with muscle when he moved. He had that glow about him that called to her, even from this distance.

"It's beautiful," Gwera breathed from beside her. She clenched her jaw and glared at the witch.

"Don't speak," she growled.

"I was only trying to figure out what was happening back home. I was doing it for you." She'd been repeating that excuse all day.

"I don't care who you thought you were doing it for. You forced me to watch my mother die." She rounded on the witch, her eyes glinting with power. "You may not have known what was going to happen but I know you. I know you've been waiting for my Fae side to emerge. I know you probably hoped the pain of seeing my mother in any weakened position would push me over the edge, that's why you dragged me through my memories of her first." She held out a hand and flames flickered over her skin, winding around her wrist before settling over her palm. "You got what you wanted and now you can live with the consequences. Do. Not. Speak. To. Me." She whirled away from the witch and stormed down the mountainside into the valley. Her anger was burning through her, clouding her mind, rolling through her veins, uninhibited.

She hated Gwera for forcing this pain to the surface.

She hated Sinisstra for stealing her kingdom and killing her parents.

She hated King Griel of Hrinth for ordering a whip down her back.

She hated Caerin for forcing her into a wild fox hunt that led her away from her kingdom and gave Sinisstra time to torture and kill her mother.

She hated the gods for choosing this fate for her, thus taking away all of her choices.

She hated Jash for starting this war.

Most importantly, she hated herself for the anger and pain and loathing she had allowed into her soul. She hated that this was who she had become, a wrathful Fae ready to burn down the world to get what she wanted. She hated that deep down, she knew she was no better than Sinisstra. But she couldn't exactly take that out on herself so she focused her rage and her hate until it became a beacon.

She would make them regret crossing her path.

Chapter 31

Caerin

The dragonslayer woke to a nudge on his leg. He groaned and rolled over to see one of the younger dragons curled up at the foot of his bed, smoke curling from its nostrils. Dragons always hatched with the ability to breathe fire, in order to protect themselves while they matured. After the juvenile stage, the fire glands stop working in all species of dragons except for wyrms and lindwurms. He sat up and ran a hand over the soft scales on its head and it hummed, pressing its head into his hand.

Something is different today, the youngling said, lifting its head.

"What is that supposed to mean?" he asked. The dragon only shook its head and stood, striding to the window before unfolding its wings and flying out into the valley. He sighed and got out of bed, dressing in his homespun cotton tunic and pants before making his way from the castle to make sure his scaly companions were taking care of themselves. One youngling had come across a particularly brave wolf and now sported a nasty gash on its flank that he wanted to check on to make sure no infection had spread.

The path. The path. The path. Every dragon he passed repeated the same two words to him and he followed their gazes to the mountain path, the only route into Greydell. Hadi had returned two days ago and she wouldn't shut up about a group of elves she had encountered on the path, one who had formed an invisible connection with her. He had hoped they were lost northerners who wouldn't make it to his small haven but as his gaze lifted to the mountainside, there was no mistaking the five figures that were making their way towards him. Two were male, most likely twins if their matching facial features and dark heads of hair were any indications. They were tall and lithe with bows strapped to their backs. One had long hair tied at the nape of his neck while the other kept his hair short, out of his face. The male with shorter hair was attached at the hip to a tall female with white-blonde hair, also kept short. It swept across her forehead in snowy wisps and there was an enormous greatsword strapped to her back. Her arms were thicker than her mate's, corded with muscle from years of wielding a sword. The smallest female had an air of grace about her with hair the same red shade as his styled in a straight blunt bob that ended just below her chin. Green wisps of magic swirled around her fingers. A witch, he realized, and a powerful one at that if her scent was to be relied on.

The last female, she was fae. She was taller than the males, though still shorter than him and her face was beautiful, regal, with high cheekbones and a sharp jaw. Her lips were full and set in a beautiful scowl as she marched towards him. She walked with an air of confidence, anger burning in her steps. Behind her, she left a trail of red flowers, a side effect of her strong emotion. She was probably young, just settling into her powers then. He found himself breathless as he gazed at her. Della had told him they would come just as she showed him how to burn away his mortal skin, but he had secretly hoped they would not come so soon. He had found peace here and hated to have that interrupted.

"Who are you and how did you find me?" he asked as they drew near enough for them to hear him. The fae woman flashed her canines but neglected to answer him before her fist cracked against his jaw.